THE PRIVATEER:

A PIRATE FOR THE QUEEN

By R.C. Andersen

Spring Publishing

SPRING PUBLISHING
P.O. Box 458
Independence, OR 97351

THE PRIVATEER: A PIRATE FOR THE QUEEN

Cover Illustration: Liz Collins

Library of Congress Catalog Number: 98-96572

ISBN: 0-9666946-0-0

First Edition: April 1999

To

Craig Johnson

A Swashbucklin' Picaroon
If Ever There Was!

THE TABLE
OF CONTENTS

1. THE CHASE   **7**

2. THE CAPTIVES   **22**

3. PORT ROYAL   **39**

4. WIDOW'S WATCH   **52**

5. THE DEAL   **61**

6. THE RIDDLE   **77**

7. GAVETTE'S ISLAND   **99**

8. NASSAU   **111**

9. BACK TO THE *BERNADETTE*   **126**

10. DOWN THE BANK   **135**

11. THE MOUTH OF THE DRAGON   **146**

12. THE AMBUSH   **163**

13. A PROMISE KEPT   **171**

14. TYBURN FAIR   **179**

chapter 1

THE CHASE

The *Bernadette*'s sails stretched full before a warm subtropic wind; her bow rose and fell in a powerful rhythm, plowing white the sky blue waves of the eastern Atlantic. The sun was high, near one o'clock. The captain of the *Bernadette*, Jacob Maxwell, stood on the quarterdeck next to his helmsman at the wheel. Maxwell's eyes were fixed on a vessel the *Bernadette* was rapidly overtaking; the whole crew was anxious for a report from Ivy Sabin, their lookout, up in his crow's nest. Could this finally be the *De la Cruz*, the ship they had been searching for all the way across the Atlantic? Time was running out! It was only a few day's sail now from the West Indies, where a French merchantman might easily find sanctuary from pursuers such as the *Bernadette*.

Up in the crow's nest, Ivy Sabin held a long brass spyglass to his good right eye; a black patch covered his blind left eye. Ivy's naked right eye could see better than any other man's two, and with his lens he could see farther than anybody ever had, drunk or sober. With his back against the mainmast, Ivy wedged his foot up snug into the nest rim to stabilize himself and his spyglass, and homed in on a name carved in grandiose letters athwart the stern of the ship running ahead. "There she flies!" he whispered triumphantly to himself, before calling down to the decks below.

"Ahoy, Cap'n Maxwell! She's the *De la Cruz* all right!"

"Hurrah!" A shout of approval erupted from all hands.

"Bring 'er near!" the captain ordered, and those not already at their posts now hurried to their stations.

Captain Maxwell took over the wheel and steered the *Bernadette* alongside the *De la Cruz*, near enough for those aboard the French galleon to see the privateer's skull and crossbones flapping boldly in the breeze atop her mainmast.

The *Bernadette* sent a cannonball screaming across the bow of the *De la Cruz*, suggesting she strike sail and prepare to be boarded.

But the French merchantman responded by raising her own Jolly Roger, and returning fire. The rebuff landed just short of the *Bernadette*'s port bow in a rude explosion of ocean spray, letting Maxwell and his men know they were going to have to earn their prize.

Captain Maxwell turned his ship windward to luff her sails and slow her.

Returning again to the wake of the *De la Cruz*, the *Bernadette*'s bow cannon started blasting away at the sails of the French pirate ship. The *De la Cruz* had no stern artillery, and her crew could be seen scrambling to set something up; but a good measure of the merchantman's canvas was in rags before a rear gun could be mounted, and by then the *Bernadette* was already approaching to starboard, her crew about to board.

First over the rail, as always, was the colossal Moon and his best mate, Spike. The greater portion of the *Bernadette* complement followed in a clamorous swarm close behind. Spike let go of the hook and rope he came swinging in on and landed at Moon's back, his feet crashing into the chest of a *De la Cruz* crewman.

"Are you ready for another lesson in the fine art of swordsmanship, Moon?" Spike shouted to his large friend, as they stood back to back, waving their swords at an angry host coming at them from all sides.

"Allow me," said Moon, and he made a mighty swing of his cutlass at the nearest Frenchman, sending the man flying backward into a throng of his mates.

"No! No! No!" scolded Spike. "That was much too

clumsy. Observe: parry, parry, stab; parry, stab." With each utterance of the word *stab*, Spike, with amazing agility, bestowed a cut onto one and then the other arm of a be-dazzled French pirate, who dropped his sword and shrank away, wailing a shrill medley of agony and astonishment.

"Oh, like this!" returned Moon. "Parry ... parry ... stab ..." The huge Moon lunged at the man now before him, a pirate who easily sidestepped the slow, awkward thrust, and countered with a swipe at Moon's head. An angered Moon reached out and grabbed the buccaneer's sword hilt in his left hand, and, using his right, lifted the howling sea dog out of his boots and tossed him over the side of the ship.

"Not quite!" laughed Spike, now engaged with a fellow surprisingly clever with a sword. Not used to the superb competition, Spike started toying with his talented op-ponent. "Very good!" he exclaimed at one point when the crafty pirate came near to slashing his ear off. Spike was a master swordsman, even the most capable Captain Jacob Maxwell was always glad to see the little Irishman on his side doing battle.

It was clear from the outset the *De la Cruz* was no match for the *Bernadette*. Maxwell led the main advance of the English privateers steadily and stalwartly abaft the hap-less galleon; and there they found the *De la Cruz* officers standing their ground, awaiting the inevitable.

"Well, well!" exclaimed Maxwell, as he deflected a couple of halfhearted sword thrusts from a French dandy dressed in green silk and white lace, jealously guarding the hatchway of the *De la Cruz* captain's cabin. "If it isn't the always engaging Captain Armand Delcarpio. Where was it we last met, Tangier?"

"Algiers! Yew good for no-thing Englishman swine!" retorted Delcarpio, swinging his sword with increased vigor but still having little effect on Maxwell, who possessed an obvious advantage over the frustrated French gentleman.

Captain Maxwell sobered up his swordplay, becoming almost stern. "Come now, you miserable rodent, lay down that blade before you hurt yourself!"

Aware that Maxwell's mild manner could turn deadly at any moment, Delcarpio threw down his weapon, but bitterly complained: "She eez my prize! How can yew do thees!"

"Quite easily, I'm afraid," said Maxwell with a nonchalant shrug of his shoulders, and he looked around the deck to make sure Delcarpio's men were following their leader's example in giving up the fight.

Maxwell turned back to his brooding adversary, who had begun twirling one end of a much too wide, thin black mustache growing out from under too long a nose. "Where is she, then?" Maxwell demanded, looking over Delcarpio's shoulder at the captain's cabin—the most likely place.

Delcarpio begrudgingly stepped aside as Maxwell approached the cabin door. After raising his fist to knock, however, he changed his mind and turned his attention instead to the battle-disheveled horde standing around the deck of the subdued *De la Cruz*. "First things first!" The captain addressed his quartermaster: "How did we do, Mr. Fenton?"

"It looks like we have two dead and a number wounded, Cap'n."

The quartermaster of a privateer was next in command after the captain and first mate. Harley Fenton saw to it that the *Bernadette* remained fit. A quartermaster was voted to his post by the crew and could be voted out at any time by the same. The captain of a privateer was also voted into power except in the rare circumstance when he owned the ship. And three years earlier, Jacob Maxwell received the *Bernadette* from the legendary pirate Captain Thatch Fitz-Henry of the good ship *Hargus*, for whom Maxwell had served many years, the last few years as first mate. The *Bernadette* was a prime English merchantman the *Hargus* had taken one day and subsequently given to Jacob Maxwell, along with his leave, as a bonus for time well served under Captain Thatch.

Shortly after awarding Maxwell the *Bernadette*, Captain Thatch retired to Madagascar to live off the bounty from many successful years of pirating the high seas.

"Two dead! In this piddle dither!" Maxwell gave Armand Delcarpio a severe stare.

Delcarpio mumbled something in French and then looked to the horizon to avoid the eyes of the perturbed Englishman.

"Let me have your ears, then!" shouted Captain Maxwell, climbing the steps to the quarterdeck of the *De la Cruz* for a better look at the battle-bedraggled lot on the main deck below. "Are there any Englishmen of the *De la Cruz* out there, willing to sign articles with the *Bernadette*—the finest ship to ever sail the high seas! It looks as if we'll be needing a few new mates."

"Four, actually," suggested Quartermaster Fenton. "Remember, we lost Glenn Flatwood to the pox, and then there was James Bigelow that disappeared."

"Right—four then!" Captain Maxwell called out to the buccaneers, several already waving their hands, eager to join the *Bernadette*. "Englishmen? Loyal to the queen?"

"Aye, sir!" rose a chorus of shouts.

Maxwell climbed back down to the main deck to survey the possibilities. "Who was it put away Toby Gant?" The captain pointed at a body being tossed over the rail.

"It was me, sir," said one of the pirates with a hand up.

"Who are you? Toby was a scrapper. You must have something to bring *him* down."

The captain called to Ivy Sabin, still in the *Bernadette*'s crow's nest, "Did you see it, Ivy?" Captain Maxwell did not wish an injury befalling his gifted lookout during a battle, so Ivy (along with the ship's white-haired doctor-cook, Emmett Sedgwick, and Emmett's young helper, Egan Shaw) remained aboard the *Bernadette* during a fight. Emmett and Egan were now going about tending to the wounded.

"It was a fair fight," proclaimed Ivy Sabin.

"John Reniker," said the man standing before Maxwell.

"No, we have a John. And I don't like Reniker. I'm giving you the name of the man you dispatched. Wear it well! He was a fine mate! Welcome aboard the *Bernadette*, Toby Gant!"

"Thank you, sir."

To eliminate confusion, no two men shared a name aboard the *Bernadette*, nor were names held that were considered bad luck or in poor form: Gold, Silver, Rain, Gale, parts of a ship, a crewman's archenemy, or any other name found objectionable by a crewman.

"There stands a fit man with a saber, Cap'n," said Spike, pointing out the fellow that had given him a good fight, who was now clasping a wound on his upper arm, compliments of Spike.

"And who might this be—to win high praise from Spike hisself?" Maxwell walked over to the solid, swarthy man, handsomely dressed in a fancy blue rag cap and purple squaretailed coat.

"Zak Drago, sir."

"You're an Englishman, Zak Drago?" Maxwell gave him the hard eye.

"I don't know what to call myself, Cap'n. I've seen many a headland, but favor none above the other."

"You can call yourself a crewman of the *Bernadette*, if you so desire."

"Thank you, sir."

"Amidships, leaning on the rail," Ivy shouted down from above, and he pointed out a short, stout, and baldheaded fellow standing with his arms crossed, who jumped to attention with surprise at the lookout's words. "That fellow put up a good fight."

"He did, now?" questioned the captain. "And who might you be?"

"Cory Heath, and it would be a *high* honor, sir!" said the pudgy man at the low end of a bow he made deliberately ridiculous; the gesture made everybody laugh.

A young man shuffled up to the captain, waving an earnest hand. "Please, sir, Captain Maxwell, sir, might I have the privilege?"

"What is this?" Maxwell surveyed the lad, who looked sturdy enough, but surely few in years. "How old are you?"

"Sixteen, sir."

"More like fourteen—at the most!"

"Please, sir, I've followed your course! And I've always desired to serve under your sail! And Captain Thatch Fitz-Henry has always been my hero!"

"He was more than a hero to me," Jacob Maxwell stated with pride, and remembered he couldn't have been much older than this lad when he had asked permission to become part of a crew, beseeching Captain Thatch to take him on.

"I would gladly serve for a half-share!" the youth offered.

"Every man aboard the *Bernadette* gets an equal share!" Maxwell said emphatically. "Except for me, a' course: I get two equal shares."

The *Bernadette* crew laughed again.

"Quartermaster and first mate get one and a half shares; helmsman, bos'n, gunner—one and a quarter. What's your name, kid?"

"Billy Fry, sir!"

"A word of wisdom, Billy Fry. Henceforth, any man calls you *kid*—this meaning me as well—you cut out his heart! Understand?" Jacob Maxwell stared hard into the eyes of Billy Fry, man to man.

"Aye, sir!"

"Welcome aboard.

"Now, what shall we do with the rest of this tangled lot? I know what to do with this one!" Maxwell made another contemptuous glare in the direction of Armand Delcarpio.

The Frenchman stopped mumbling momentarily to glance at his captor with a squinty eye.

Captain Maxwell raised his voice, his eyes still on Delcarpio:"Kipp, you and Depwig ready the longboat.

"Zak Drago!"

The new recruit hurried to the captain's side.

"You and Wesley Tuttle here"—Maxwell reached out and grabbed the shoulder of one of his men—"gather up Monsieur Delcarpio and his closest mates, and bring 'em round amidships."

Maxwell walked back over to the captain's cabin hatchway of the *De la Cruz*, and raised his hand to knock, but once again stopped himself, and started pacing back and forth, scratching his chin, deep in thought.

And then the captain came to a halt, and smiled, and was about to say something—but changed his mind and resumed pacing, back and forth, back and forth.

Zak Drago and Wesley Tuttle finished bringing Captain Delcarpio and his officers together; Maxwell noticed this and blew a sigh of relief as he rejoined them.

"Well done." The captain also saw that the longboat was ready to be lowered. "And well done," he complimented Kipp Rafferty and Brice Depwig.

Quartermaster Fenton, along with Gunner Sheck

Tilley, arrived with a longboat sail they had found in one of the forecastle lockers.

"Over the side with ye, then!" ordered Captain Maxwell.

The captain of the French pirates and his officers were lowered to sea in the longboat amid loud jeers and tauntings from the victorious *Bernadette* crew.

As Maxwell watched the distraught Frenchmen push off the side of their former ship and struggle at rigging sail to the overcrowded boat as it bobbed up and down on the rolling swells, he wondered what he was going to do with the *De la Cruz*. Normally they would escort a captured vessel to a friendly port in the Caribbean and trade her off. But this could not be done with the *De la Cruz*; the *Bernadette* had to distance herself from this leaky barrel. Every pirate ship, privateer, and military ship on the Atlantic was on the lookout for this one, because of her cargo—the cargo Maxwell was trying to avoid dealing with for as long as he could.

"Until zee next time, yew Englishman swine!" Delcarpio shouted and shook his fist in the air as the longboat's sail filled with wind, heading for the West Indies, somewhere beyond the horizon.

"There were but a few trinkets in the treasure store," said Quartermaster Fenton, reporting what he and Tilley had found below. "And the timbers are honeycombed with teredo worm and weed."

"Aye, she's a sorry piece of driftwood," grumbled Maxwell, regarding the dilapidated *De la Cruz*. He then called out, for all to hear: "Anybody care to buy a fine French schooner?" And he slapped the starboard rail of the old merchantman to suggest a soundness that wasn't there.

"That's a funny joke, sir, as if we would be able —after you've taken your spoils," complained a *De la Cruz* crewman.

Maxwell spread a wily grin. "But here's the deal, lad, and a fine one, too. We let you keep the *De la Cruz*, and then afterwards—that is, in the future, after you've won a good stake and our bows cross once more—you hand over five hundred pieces of eight."

A short silence ensued, followed by some grumbling and sneers and a great deal of head shaking on the part of the defeated stragglers.

Maxwell coughed. "We're speaking of *silver* eight, a' course," he clarified, after seeing his original proposal received so unkindly. Insisting the money was silver and not gold was lowering the price seven-ninths.

"She's a weary old tub, Cap'n," said an old, well-salted French pirate, shaking his head.

"Three hundred—and that's my final offer, or we'll just set fire to 'er and let 'er scuttle! You can't buy a dinghy for three hundred!"

The grumbling recommenced as this offer was also received less than heartily.

"One fifty seems more in line," said a voice in the crowd; the greater portion of the *De la Cruz* complement nodded their heads in agreement.

"I don't believe this! One fifty is absolutely laughable!" Maxwell spun on his heels as he drew his sword and then pressed the tip of the shimmering steel up against the belly of the nearest Frenchman. "Two hundred is too little, but we'll take it because we are such a generous, good-hearted lot."

The majority of the *De la Cruz* crew shrugged their shoulders in resignation, reluctantly accepting the deal. This triggered another burst of laughter from the *Bernadette* crew.

"Two hundred in silver, then, the next time we meet."

Jacob Maxwell returned to the hatchway of the *De la Cruz* captain's cabin. He raised his hand, hesitated one last time, and then, after being unable to think of another excuse, knocked.

When an answer was not forthcoming, he knocked again, louder this time.

Another interval of quiet followed.

The captain banged his fist on the door, shouting, "Open up in there!"

But silence again held sway.

"Moon," the captain ordered, "break her down."

Moon stepped up and put his shoulder to it and the door flew open.

From inside the cabin, female voices shrieked.

Maxwell ran into the cabin, sword in hand. When he heard the women scream, he thought one of Delcarpio's men had stowed himself inside and was about to dispose of the women in spite; but after finding only two females cowering in a corner, the captain sheathed his saber.

Jacob Maxwell had contemplated long and hard about what he was going to do when this moment finally arrived. And now he bowed, and declared: "Captain Jacob Maxwell, loyal subject of Queen Elizabeth, at your service, Your Ladyship."

chapter 2

THE CAPTIVES

Sarah Howard, the third child of Anne, who at one time had been the first cousin twice removed and next in line to the throne of Queen Catherine Howard, whose head was once removed by King Henry VIII, came out of the corner with her girl servant, both attempting to look less rattled than they were.

Sarah Howard's life had changed dramatically with the announcement by her cousin, Queen Elizabeth, of Sarah's engagement to Albert Dudley. The news came as a surprise to Sarah; she had met her betrothed but once (Albert's face remained a blur no matter how hard she tried to conjure it up!), during a royal reception of some sort (there had been so many!). Her initial fiery opposition to the arranged marriage began to cool when she became the toast of the Netherlands, where she had been visiting some Dutch friends at the time of the royal decree. Sarah immediately became the darling of every gathering, the recipient of countless congratulatory gifts and invitations to dine.

Albert Dudley was the next to the last son of the late and only brother of Lord Robert Dudley, who was presently the Earl of Leicester and faithful companion to Her Royal Highness, the Virgin Queen Elizabeth.

One evening, while sipping wine and discussing domestic matters before the royal bedroom fireplace, the Virgin Queen and her companion came to decide that it was time Robert's mischievous nephew got married; this would, they hoped, settle the restless Albert and put some responsibility and direction into an obviously aimless existence.

Sarah had come to enjoy her transformation from wallflower to radiant rose; and she was happily on her way back to England to be formally introduced to her future husband, when her ship was overrun by the revolting French pirate Armand Delcarpio, in a barbaric and altogether unchivalrous attack at sea.

Her Ladyship had hardly come to terms with her humiliating captivity when the ship in which she is being held prisoner is attacked—by more pirates!

And then comes the breaking down of her door by officers of the Royal Navy! Disguised as pirates!?

"So you are actually an officer in Her Majesty's Navy?" inquired Sarah of Jacob Maxwell, after he had respectfully offered his services to her.

"Er . . . not exactly, ma'am."

"Then who are you—what are you? I don't understand!" Sarah took a fan away from her girl servant and began stirring the air vigorously before her flushed cheeks and brow.

Maxwell watched Sarah's attendant—who appeared to be slightly younger than Sarah and every bit as lovely—usher Her Ladyship into a chair at the captain's table in the middle of the cabin, and then produce a second fan to help cool her mistress.

"I am, I should say, we are privateers under the commission of Lord Brackenbough of New Hampshire," explained Maxwell.

"You *are* a pirate, then!" Sarah swooned, worry again apparently overwhelming her.

"Privateer, ma'am."

"It's all the same, isn't it! Pirate, privateer, criminal! I suppose I am now *your* prisoner!"

"A pirate holds no allegiance, Your Ladyship. My men and I are loyal subjects of England and the queen."

This was a sore spot with Jacob Maxwell, and with all privateers for that matter; it was an insult to call a privateer a pirate. But there was good reason for Sarah's concern, both the pirate and the privateer were self-serving marauders of the high seas. The only real difference between a pirate and a privateer was that the privateer had permission from England to rob the Spanish. A percentage of the booty obtained by a privateer supposedly went to the British crown, usually through an agent in the American colonies. In fact, the court representative, who was often the governor of a colony, required an annual fee for a commission and only a small portion of the queen's share of loot actually found its way to England. However, the crown was much less interested in the financial gain brought about by the privateering enterprise than in the pleasure they received by harassing Spain—England's archenemy.

The most prized commission was one obtained directly from the queen, with her insignia on the document. A regular commission was easy enough to come by in the colonies, for a price, but it had little credibility outside the New World. A queen's commission was held by only the most esteemed entrepreneur, usually a former naval or military officer. A bearer of a queen's commission was looked upon in nearly the same light as an active naval officer: minor nobility. He had permission to take his booty home to England and present it personally to the crown, and then spend his share however he pleased, anywhere on English soil.

A regular commission holder, on the other hand, was regarded by the crown as a necessary inconvenience. He was expected to keep his distance from Her Majesty and

England, and was not to bring an embarrassment home to a queen and country that were outwardly assuring the rest of the world that no such enterprise existed. (The document itself being a vaguely worded business agreement with little hint as to its true purpose.)

A queen's commission was sometimes given as a reward for an outstanding service rendered or heroic deed done; this is what brought Captain Maxwell and the *Bernadette* to the aid of Sarah Howard. By rescuing the queen's cousin, Jacob Maxwell was hoping to obtain a queen's commission.

"I assure you, ma'am, it is our deepest desire to carry you safely back to England. Your good health is of our utmost concern." Captain Maxwell ordered his men out of the cabin, returning some privacy to the ladies. He then sat down opposite the anxious royal; that is, Maxwell sat down after removing his sword, which he forgot he was wearing and slammed into the table in his initial attempt at sitting down.

"Yes, indeed, it gets a bit muggy at these latitudes," the captain said, drumming his fingers impatiently on the tabletop, trying to think of a way to calm Sarah, watching her and the girl servant fanning the royal countenance— and a right pretty face it was!

"Muggy?" asked Sarah, distracted momentarily from her distress. "What is 'muggy'?"

"Muggy? The climate, ma'am. It makes one hot and, er . . ." Maxwell was about to use the word *sweaty* but thought it likely too crude a word for royal ears; instead, using a fingertip, he wiped some sweat from his forehead and presented it to Her Ladyship.

"Perspiration. Yes, it does do that!" Sarah panted, increasing the speed of her fan.

Looking around the cabin, Maxwell could see why the *De la Cruz*'s treasure store was found so wanting: a marvelous assortment of fineries had been hung, draped, and laid about the room. The Carp must have really put himself out in accommodating his royal prisoner. "It looks like Monsieur Delcarpio has spruced up the cabin a mite."

"This drabble!" Sarah exclaimed, putting down her fan as she got up from the table. She walked over to a shelf overflowing with valuables, and picked up a lampshade sitting beside an elegant gold-framed portrait of a dull, sapless gentleman in uniform. Removing a necklace and string of pearls dangling from the lampshade, Sarah looked around the roomful of curiosities as if searching for a lamp to put the shade on—or another shade to hang the jewelry from. "This! It is so . . . so . . . uncoordinated!"

"Yes, well, you'll find the *Bernadette* far more accommodating, you can be sure of that," said Captain Maxwell with a nod.

"Back to England—home, you say?" inquired Sarah,

seeking further reassurance that the rescue was indeed real.

It was no small task transferring the women and their belongings to the captain's cabin of the *Bernadette*. And most of Maxwell's things had to be removed to the crew's quarters. There was no shortage of volunteers in assisting the ladies, however. Particularly enthusiastic were Egan Shaw and Billy Fry. The two young men were falling all over themselves in their quest for the obligation of Sarah's attendant, Rebecca Webb.

"I guess we now know the reason Billy Fry was so eager to sign on with the *Bernadette*," said Emmett Sedgwick, the *Bernadette*'s doctor-cook, between draws on his corn-cob pipe. He and the captain watched Billy stagger under a large chest he was carrying.

"I'd say young Egan has a motive of his own." Maxwell pointed a thumb at Emmett's assistant, who had just stumbled on a coil of twine in his efforts at helping Rebecca onto the temporary rope bridge connecting the two ships. "There is only one thing more disruptive aboard ship than a pretty woman."

"Aye, and that would be *two* pretty women," joked Emmett.

"All we need now is a keg of rum," said the captain, referring to the havoc women and strong drink were known to bring a vessel.

"But this is a good cause! A just end!" said the wise old doctor-cook, taking his pipe from his mouth to stab the air and emphasize his point. "There'll be good luck a' comin' from this, you'll see!"

The *Bernadette* left the *De la Cruz* and her crew to their fates, and continued on for the West Indies, intending to make a short stopover in the islands before returning Sarah as expeditiously as possible to England.

* * *

As soon as the *De la Cruz* was found, it would be the *Bernadette*'s turn at being the prize catch of the sea, the target of a great many vessels and men aiming to increase their fortunes. Come supper time that evening, Captain Maxwell settled a bit uneasily into his chair, thinking about his increase in status as a renegade. But what was making the captain even more uncomfortable was the empty plate on the food-laden table before him, and the eating utensils lying in wait on both sides of the dish. He had seen their like before and knew their purpose, but up to this point in his life, Jacob Maxwell had never executed the appropriate operation. He knew the task was twofold: first, use a certain tool to bring the eatables from the table to his plate; and second, use another tool to reduce the size of the portion on the plate before hauling it to

THE PRIVATEER: A PIRATE FOR THE QUEEN

his mouth. And, of most importance, all this had to be done with a minimum of spillage!

Sarah's servant, Rebecca, came to his rescue regarding the first part of the problem. "Allow me, sir." She filled his plate with boiled potatoes, corned beef and cabbage, and applesauce. Jacob took note that Rebecca had left a large bowl of fruit and nuts, set in the middle of the table, undisturbed; perhaps this was to be regarded as a decoration, similar to an arrangement of flowers.

"That is a handsome bowl of fruit and nuts," said the captain.

"I found a grand assortment down below," said Rebecca. "Egan Shaw showed me a whole roomful of crates and barrels of foodstuff."

"Thank Emmett Sedgwick for that, a fine cook hisself. He's also the ship's surgeon, and Egan his helper." Maxwell was wondering what to do now with what was on his plate; he decided to follow the ladies' example—do as they did—but they seemed more intent on talking than eating.

"So you and that dreadful Captain Delcarpio know each other?" inquired Sarah, holding a knife idly in one hand; a fork likewise lay listless in the other.

"We know *of* each other, you might say," Maxwell replied while copying Sarah's choice of utensils.

The captain, Her Ladyship, and Her Ladyship's attendant: all three sat motionless before the meal. The ladies wished the captain to expound upon his comment; the captain was waiting for somebody to make the required maneuver. Then Jacob came to realize what the ladies wanted.

"It was in Nassau I first had dealings with the ornery little Frenchman," Maxwell said, laying down his knife and fork. He scratched his chin and took mental note of the eating methods now being employed by the ladies.

"The Carp—that is the nickname we men of the sea use in referring to the gentleman—is most handy with the cards, and that was how he made his stake. I was still under Cap'n Thatch's sail at the time . . ."

"Captain Thatch Fitz-Henry? You sailed with Captain Thatch Fitz-Henry!" exclaimed Rebecca. "That must have been exciting!"

"Rebecca!" scolded Sarah. "He was a dreadful pirate, a scoundrel!"

"Begging your pardon, ma'am," insisted the former first mate of the *Hargus*, "Captain Thatch flew no flag but his own, that's a fact, but there was no more fair nor just man under the clouds! He'd stand by a mate till his last hair, he would!" Maxwell had to restrain himself while correcting Her Ladyship; he knew she meant no real harm, but if Sarah had been a man, she would be, by now, lying in several pieces at his feet.

Jacob Maxwell was proud the ladies knew of his dear old captain and mentor; he couldn't help, however, being a little disappointed that they had never heard of him; Captain Jacob Maxwell was certainly known on the high seas, and no doubt at most ports—but how far inland by the common folk? Maxwell picked up a knife and poked at the corned beef on his plate.

"So you played cards with the Carp?" prodded Rebecca.

"What? Not me! I know a cheat when one's about." A younger Jacob Maxwell had actually lost a hefty sum of gold and silver coin before realizing that something had to be amiss regarding the better than average luck of the Frenchman. "And Nassau was full of 'em back then, and still is for that matter—most of 'em mates of Delcarpio, one time or another."

Maxwell managed to slice and deliver a few bites of beef to his mouth, using his fork, without dropping any in his lap. He was pleased with himself and tried the applesauce, exchanging his fork for his spoon after seeing that it would hold more; before this evening Maxwell had always drunk his applesauce from a mug.

"We ran into the Carp at Maracaibo a while back. I think that's where he got his hands on the *De la Cruz*. He should've stuck with cards; had a number of ships under his boots and hasn't yet hung on to any of them for long." Maxwell laughed, remembering some of Delcarpio's misfortunes, having had a hand in many of them. "And then there was Caracas and Port Royal, of course." Maxwell and his men had dealt with the French pirate captain at other times and places, but none recently or otherwise worthy of mention at the moment. "That's where we'll be landing in a day or two."

"Port Royal?" inquired Sarah, concern in her voice.

"Yes, ma'am."

"I've heard it is a dreadful and lawless place—a pirate's den!"

"The home of many a pirate, that's true enough, I suppose. But lawless? No, ma'am. There are plenty of laws to go around, and they're all obeyed to the letter. If not, it's the last law a man disregards. The same punishment holds for any and all crimes committed at Port Royal—and the reason why a man seldom runs aground. Port Royal is a lively place, but rarely is a law ignored." Maxwell took a long drink from his mug and then used his sleeve to wipe away a small trickle of wine wandering down his chin. He blushed slightly after doing so, remembering his manners. Then he stopped himself—just in time—from belching.

"What is the punishment?" asked Rebecca.

"The cage, ma'am."

"Oh yes!" Rebecca's face crinkled in a grimace as she recalled, "We saw a poor man in one of those on the

Thames, as we were leaving London for Holland."

The cage was just that: a small iron-bar cage with just enough room for a man to stand in. It was lowered into a harbor so water rose to the prisoner's chin come high tide. The condemned man was left to slowly waste away, to dissolve in the salty brine that at first stung the wounds made by the bites of small sea creatures, and then, after death, wore away his flesh until only the skeleton and tattered clothing of the criminal remained. A doomed man was well advised to drink the seawater he was submerged in to quicken his death by poisoning (a painful but shorter death, involving an intense cramping of all his body's muscles) or else drown himself.

The magistrates of a port city often directed that prisoners and their cages be attached to the hazard bouys of the city's harbor so the moaning of the condemned men might act as an additional warning for incoming vessels to avoid submerged rocks, wrecks, and other obstructions. This was especially useful at night, and in a fog.

The cage had been introduced to Port Royal during her early stages of development. Everyone agreed the cage had become necessary to inhibit the inherently unruly bent of Port Royal's inhabitants and guests. Minor infractions of the rules were naturally ignored, but major trespasses were dealt with in a manner befitting a community that preferred little policing and even less rehabilitation.

After Sarah had eaten her fill of what was on her plate, she took a pear from the bowl of fruit and nuts in the middle of the table and began peeling the skin with a knife.

Rebecca followed with the choice of a large, shiny red apple, taking a big bite and not minding the skin.

This is more like it! thought Maxwell. This was how eating was meant to be done, hand to mouth. He grabbed two walnuts and crushed them together in his hand. This was something Maxwell had done countless times without thinking about what he was doing and without the least flaw in technique; he would simply crush two walnuts together in his left hand and pick the meat out with the fingers of his right hand. He had done this more times than he could remember, without anything ever going awry, with nothing out of the ordinary ever happening— until this evening: when Jacob crushed the two walnuts together, a large piece of shell went flying across the table and hit Rebecca's half-empty wine goblet.

Cling!

The sound reverberated around the cabin, creating a moment of freezing embarrassment.

Recovering his aplomb, the captain joked, "Actually, I was aiming at your apple."

Rebecca looked at her apple and laughed. Sarah also couldn't help but giggle.

"How did you learn that Monsieur Delcarpio had taken us hostage?" Sarah asked.

"We heard about it in The Hague. After the deed was done, everybody knew, a' course. And some of his crew were tellin' tales beforehand in Morocco, where a good many ships were musterin' for the attack on Brest. The *Bernadette* and some other privateers were enlisted by Captain Jennings of Her Majesty's Navy, to help settle a score down there."

The French and the English had hated each other long before the Spanish came into their own with the fabulous wealth they wrenched from the New World. Under a Spain-dominated Europe, for many decades, the French and the English allied themselves against a common adversary. But this did not put an end to the many ongoing feuds between factions of the two rivals, separated by only a few miles of English Channel. Battles—if not small wars—were waged here and there on land or sea without a formal declaration of hostilities by the head of state of either country. Privateers and pirates were commonly employed when an action was required on or by sea.

Aaron Jennings was a naval officer with many ties with privateers and pirates. He was one of a few that did the recruiting when some form of unsavory service was needed on the side of the English.

To take part in the Battle of Brest, Captain Maxwell

had requested a queen's commission. Jennings agreed to try to procure one for Maxwell, even though he knew it was impossible; Queen Elizabeth loathed Jennings and would never agree to see him, let alone grant a commission to someone on his recommendation.

But Jennings led Maxwell on in order to obtain the *Bernadette*'s services, which proved instrumental in the victory at Brest. After the battle, Jennings left Maxwell waiting in Holland as he pretended to go back to London and solicit the queen on Maxwell's behalf.

Holland managed to remain neutral at a time when all the countries around her bickered and fought. She was consistently the only haven in Europe for a ship regardless of the flag the ship flew. The Netherlands used her peaceful indifference to her advantage, gleaning tremendous wealth at the expense of her quarreling neighbors.

As the *Bernadette* was preparing to depart Holland's port city The Hague, after getting disappointing news from Jennings that a queen's commisson had been denied, Maxwell learned that Captain Armand Delcarpio had made good on his threat to take Sarah Howard; here was another opportunity to gain favor with the crown.

" . . . And a fine meal it was," said Captain Maxwell at the door, as he was about to take leave of Her Ladyship. This matter of dining etiquette wasn't the knotty task Jacob had dreaded it might be—once you got the hang of it. He would have preferred to skip the meal, but it was his duty as captain to join Sarah Howard at her first dinner aboard. This was the first time he had entertained a woman on the *Bernadette*, although it was actually Rebecca Webb who prepared the meal. And it had been Sarah who had asked *him* to join *her* that evening.

"Feel free to go about the *Bernadette*, but try not to get underfoot the men at their duties, especially in a gale, which I don't foresee anytime soon." Jacob smiled and kissed the hand of Sarah Howard. "Ladies," he declared, before departing.

Sarah and Rebecca smiled at each other as they listened to the captain's footsteps fade from their hearing.

"Certainly a handsome enough fellow!" Rebecca whispered slyly, and giggled.

And Sarah returned, "But what appalling table manners!"

chapter 3

PORT ROYAL

Captain Maxwell paused at the ship's rail and looked out across the broad Atlantic Ocean that was fast becoming the Caribbean Sea. The moon was almost full, the warm wind steady; he judged the *Bernadette* to reach Jamaica and Port Royal in a few days, if the fair weather held.

The captain breathed a sigh of relief for having survived dining with Sarah Howard and her companion. He thought of his earlier concerns about transporting the royal cargo, when he had been in favor of holding Sarah Howard prisoner, locked in the jug until the *Bernadette* could deliver her safely home. This would have kept the queen's cousin isolated from the crew and prevented giving her an opportunity to display some high and mighty airs.

Growing up a street urchin forced to live by his wits

round about London's squalid lanes, Jacob Maxwell had felt the upper hand of the ruling class on too many occasions. The captain regretted having his authority, and so his vessel, put in jeopardy by recognizing Sarah Howard as Her Ladyship and her status as being above his own. He mistrusted and hated the aristocracy. His desire for a queen's commission had nothing to do with becoming a court favorite; he wanted the document simply for the added advantages it offered.

It was Emmett Sedgwick, his doctor-cook, who talked Maxwell into playing his hand straight—if not altogether honestly. "As long as we're at sea, under sail, everybody knows who the captain is, Her Ladyship included," Emmett had insisted. "A woman is a different creature than a leather-necked man . . . and a handsome fella like you!" Here the ship's surgeon had given Jacob an elbow to the ribs. What did he mean by that? Jacob Maxwell knew absolutely nothing about proper ladies, having mingled only with barmaids of port cities.

Thinking about his doctor-cook must have reminded his stomach of food, for it now growled. Maxwell was hungry; he hadn't eaten much at table where he had been more concerned with his performance than with what or how much he was eating. Jacob started across the deck toward the forward hatch, wondering what Emmett had on the stove.

"Hey! Break it up!" Maxwell heard Moon shout in the dark somewhere near the stern water barrel. The captain could also hear the grunts and groans of a scuffle. He watched Moon reach down and lift Egan Shaw and Billy Fry up off the deck by the backs of their necks, their hands at each other's throats.

"Break it up!" ordered Maxwell, coming near.

The two young men pushed at each other, and they both would have fallen over backward if Moon hadn't been holding them by their shirt collars.

"What are you two about?" Maxwell demanded.

"Nothin'," said Egan.

"Well, now, you know there's only one thing I tolerate less than fighting aboard my ship, and that's doing nothin'! Ain't that so, Moon!"

"That is so, Cap'n," said Moon.

The captain started pacing back and forth, gathering a storm. "There ain't nothin' that riles me more than seein' one of my men going about doin' nothin'! It gets me in a rage, it does!" Maxwell put his face into Billy Fry's. "And here I come upon two of 'em, in the very act, and doin' a right smart job of it!

"Moon, have you ever seen a grander display of nothin' bein' done?"

"A most terrible thing, Captain," replied Moon. He was standing behind the two lads, still holding them by their collars, so they couldn't see his smile.

Captain Maxwell now turned on Egan Shaw. "Maybe I heard it wrong! What was it again? What was it you two were about?"

Egan shrugged his shoulders, sighed, and then, in a subdued voice, confessed: "Billy said Rebecca's eyes were blue."

"It's Rebecca's eyes, is it? Now we're making sense, aren't we, Moon?"

"Aye, sir!"

Maxwell had noticed, but was ignoring, an increasing number of crewmen gathering around to watch the goings on. Concerned with the disruption the two women might cause on his ship, Maxwell now saw an opportunity to further inspire his crew in respecting his orders concerning the matter. He would use Egan and Billy as an example.

"And what did Egan say was the color of Rebecca's eyes?" Maxwell demanded of Billy.

"Hazel, but they ain't, they're . . ."

"I've just come from dining with the young lady, where she was sitting right across the table from your dear captain. Staring at me wide-eyed the whole time, she was. I got a splendid look at the color!

"Would you like to know the color of Rebecca Webb's eyes, Moon?"

"I would indeed, sir."

"Ruby red! Deep and glorious! As slippery as the Irrawaddy Stone itself! Whadda-ya-thing-a-that?" The captain stared hard at Egan, and then Billy.

The two young men said nothing.

"So now you know, and if anybody else needs to know the color of Rebecca Webb's eyes, you be sure and tell 'em. Now, be off! And be doin' a little less a' nothin' from now on, or I'll keelhaul the both of you!"

After Egan and Billy had gone their separate ways, Moon whispered to his captain, "What *is* the color of her eyes, Cap'n?"

Maxwell growled and stomped off, conveying his displeasure with the episode to Moon and the other men. But their captain did think about the question, and found he couldn't remember what color Rebecca's eyes were. The color of Sarah Howard's eyes easily came to mind, however; they were a delicate blue, almost gray—the color of the mist on a morning that can't decide whether to offer a wind or remain still.

* * *

Port Royal of Jamaica and Nassau on New Providence were the major pirate havens in the New World. Nassau tolerated visits from pirates for the sake of trade, but Port Royal was completely dominated by the outlaws of the sea. Port Royal had been founded by pirates and remained theirs to do with as they saw fit. Port Royal was not unlike most of the other port cities in the Caribbean, except for a few of her laws—and the method used to enforce her laws. Swordplay, for example, was not allowed in Port Royal; fighting had to be done hand to hand and one man against one.

And the cage was the remedy for all social ills, large and small.

Entering any port city is a homecoming for a sailor, but this was particularly true of pirates heading into Port Royal during the time of the buccaneers. The crew of the *Bernadette* came running on deck when Ivy shouted his sighting of Jamaica; several of the lads had family in Port Royal.

To escape the drudgery of life on a farm, many a pretty country lass ran away from home to become a barmaid in a port city, seeking the good money and a chance at capturing a successful pirate. Most all wives of pirates living in Port Royal were former barmaids. Pirates' wives were a society unto themselves, mistresses of fine homes on the hills surrounding the bay. And it was the duty of every pirate's wife—once she became a pirate's wife—to belittle the saloons and inns down along the harbor, and strive to keep her husband from them.

As the *Bernadette* entered the mouth of Port Royal harbor, she came upon two cages chained to the coral reef, a man's head in each. One head bobbed up and down with the swells, lifeless; the other head wobbled slowly but still under its own power, its eyes looking up hazily at the *Bernadette* as she eased by.

"Who goes there?" inquired Captain Maxwell, as he looked over the rail along with the rest of his men, at the prisoner still alive.

"That's Shell Haylock!" exclaimed Kipp Rafferty, a hint of pleasure in his voice. The rest of the crew whistled and smiled in surprised recognition. Shell Haylock was a scoundrel, infamous not only for his cruel disposition but also for his uncanny ability to evade justice. The hated man had left a long zigzagging trail of extortion and dupery, bringing ruin most everywhere he went.

"So 'tis!" exclaimed Maxwell. "Who's your mate, Haylock?"

"Paddy Nor, a fine mate," said the reduced man in the cage, speaking hoarsely through cracked lips heavy with thirst. The despicable Shell Haylock tried unsuccessfully to smile. "How's about some clean water, sir?"

"To hell with you!" shouted Kipp. "And extra deep for bringing down Paddy. He was a dimwit, but he had a good heart!"

"A misunderstanding, I'm sure," said Haylock, giving his head a shake, trying to focus his thoughts. "Bring me aboard and I'll tell ye tales of gold and redemption. God is my witness!" Haylock's cage was fading astern, the *Bernadette* fast passing it by. The doomed man stuck an arm through the bars of his prison and reached out his hand as if to grab the rudder of the *Bernadette* and keep her from getting away. In a desperate, raspy voice, he insisted: "A mountain of gold! I swear it! I'll give it to you all!"

"God have mercy on your evil self, Shell Haylock. You best drink up and be done with it," answered Captain Maxwell.

"Storms and rock pinnacles!" Haylock cursed, and he filled his mouth with seawater and spit it at the *Bernadette*.

It was bad luck to be cursed by a condemned man only if he was innocent, but that didn't stop a chill from running up the spines of the *Bernadette* crew; most of them crossed themselves and spit back, just in case.

There were more than the usual number of ships anchored in Port Royal harbor, and in the mast forest there roosted the *Rhinehart*, her captain being Russell Gavette, Jacob Maxwell's archenemy. Maxwell's men looked to their leader for a reaction as the *Bernadette* glided by the seemingly empty *Rhinehart*—her crew most likely in town.

Maxwell feigned indifference and ignored the attention of his crew. "Ready the anchor," he called out, as he conned his ship to moor.

* * *

Sheck Tilley showed his teeth to a piece of broken mirror set inside three bent and rusting nails on the wall of his berth in the crew's quarters; he used his dagger to pick at a shred of tobacco lodged between two front nippers. Sheck and his mates were getting ready to go ashore; the *Bernadette* was laying over for just this one night, so the men were going to have to get the most out of the afternoon and evening. Below decks was all astir with crewmen hurrying about composing themselves. Sheck had already changed into his best waistcoat and trousers, and was impatiently waiting for the others.

"Shake it, you swabs! Time's a'wastin'! All the drink'll be drunk and all the barmaids nabbed! I'm off—" Sheck pretended to go for the hatch ladder.

"Not yet!" his mates implored him. Usually it was just his best mate Kipp Rafferty who would accompany Sheck on his bar hops, but this time ashore it seemed like everybody was desiring his company. Sheck reckoned it was most likely a safety in numbers concern, with so many ships being in port; Sheck was a pretty good scrapper, everybody knew that.

"It's too bad about Paddy Nor," said Kipp, finally ready to go. "But we warned him, didn't we—about Haylock at Alberton! Think there's any truth in that mountain of gold he was speaking of?"

"Haylock was . . . is . . . a scoundrel, full of bilge and blather!" said Sheck. "That mountain of gold is a mountain of lies and a curse if it be true! We ought to row out to his cage right now and stand over the louse till he's done in proper by the crabs!"

It took three of the *Bernadette*'s bumboats two trips to ferry Sheck Tilley and his tagalongs ashore. The main street of Port Royal was alive with buccaneers making the most of their leaves. Sheck recognized sailors from the *Bristol*, the *Eckland*, and the *Fairchild*; Kipp pointed out Morris Biggs of the *Catlow*; and there was Gus Rockwood of the *Mary Ann*. Gus was one to avoid after he'd had a few; he was now in a roped-off section of a side street, naked to his waist, boxing a professional and getting the worst of the blows. The crowd around the ring had men shouting encouragement to the drunken pirate to stay up another round while just as many others were yelling at him to fall.

The hot and dusty streets of Port Royal were made of clay and smelled of sizzling fat and onion, dog's hair, chicken feathers, horse manure. . . .

Sheck Tilley led his troops through the swinging doors of Barnacle Bob's Inn—the best place to start an afternoon of carousing. At the bar, they ordered rum and waited for their eyes to adjust to the dim lamplight. There were tables for eating, for drinking, and for playing games of dice and muggins. There was a dance floor. A corner for darts. The barmaids were outnumbered this afternoon more than usual; the loveliest of them abandoned a sailor at one of the tables and sashayed over to the bar.

"Kipp Rafferty! Is that you? When did the *Bernadette* get in?" The pretty barmaid gave Sheck Tilley a quizzical glance as she snuggled up to Kipp.

"Evelyn, my love!" said Kipp. "Are you a sight for sore eyes!"

"And so where's Steph?" asked Sheck, looking around the inn.

Sheck's question puzzled Evelyn Brauck, and she was about to say something in return, but hesitated when she noticed one of Sheck's mates with a finger to his lips, signaling her to say nothing. What was going on? The others were looking at her, too, begging her with their eyes not to spoil the fun. Evelyn decided to go along with the lads and see where things went. She shrugged her shoulders. "Stephanie? I don't know."

"What's the story with Shell Haylock and Paddy Nor?" asked Kipp, to change the subject.

"Got in a fight outside the Crown, beat somebody up. It was two against one so they got the cage," said Evelyn. "And good riddance to the devil and his idiot!"

"Paddy Nor wasn't so bad," said Kipp.

"Haylock turned the fool into his fetch dog," said Barnacle Bob from behind the bar. "He became a nuisance and had to go, along with his master."

"Well, here's to the old Paddy Nor," said Sheck, raising his glass. "May his soul rest easy."

"Tell us about you and Paddy and that mix with the Spanish at Cordoba," suggested Kipp.

Sheck retold the story, of how he and Paddy and some other lads once undertook a raid on the Acapulco-Veracruz mule train. He was halfway into the telling—where the log he and Paddy were clinging to broke apart in the rapids at Orizaba—when the former Stephanie Rollins appeared at the swinging doors of Barnacle Bob's Inn.

"Sheck Tilley!" she called out.

"Ohhh," Sheck stammered, his head beginning to spin. Forgotten images from a drunken spree began flooding his confused mind. "Steph?" he questioned, the color in his face draining.

"And who else? And why are you hanging about at Bob's?"

Sheck had always been fond of Stephanie Rollins, and toward the end of his previous leave he got so awfully drunk and happy with her he agreed to marriage. But when he awoke aboard the *Bernadette* the next day, back out on the ocean—nowhere near land—and with a throbbing head he wished on his worst enemy, Sheck Tilley bing head he wished on his worst enemy, Sheck Tilley had no idea he was a married man.

Sheck gave himself a rap on the forehead. This explained why Kipp and the other lads had kept on him for weeks, asking him if he could remember anything about what he had done in Port Royal while in his drunkenness. Once he caught Kipp winking at Link Spivey when asking the question. Sheck had figured he must have done something outstanding.

But marry Stephanie Rollins!

Sheck was overwhelmed by the images now flooding his confused mind. "I was just having a few drinks with the lads," was the only thing Sheck could think to say.

Kipp and the others exploded with laughter, slapping their thighs, collapsing to the floor.

"Well, you've had your fun, now it's time you come home," said Mrs. Tilley.

His mates waved goodbye to Sheck from the porch of Barnacle Bob's as Stephanie led her man up the hill to their home, to the house she had bought with money that Sheck left her on his return to sea, with the money he had thought he lost on dice and muggins.

chapter 4

WIDOW'S WATCH

Jacob Maxwell began climbing the steep, winding path to a tall, gray, wind-buffeted and sun-baked house sitting on the highest and most eastern point of the ridge surrounding Port Royal. The Widow's Watch sat alone on its hill, isolated from smaller houses huddled together on lesser mounds below. Atop the eastern summit, perched on the edge of the cliffs above the shantytown, the bay and the sea, dwelled the old Widow Archer, wife of the late best mate of Captain Thatch Fitz-Henry.

Winston Archer had died fighting in a raid on a Spanish galleon just short of a year after he and Fitz-Henry had gone off to sea together. The news of her husband's death had been a severe blow to Kristina Archer; she grew thin and feebleminded.

When Thatch Fitz-Henry became a prosperous pirate captain, he sent one of his men to inquire about his late partner's widow; and the man found Kristina wandering the back roads of Cornwall, speaking in riddles and swatting at invisible evils hovering overhead. Captain Thatch took the wracked woman to Port Royal and set her up in a house he had recently built for himself, and he hired a crew to look after the widow during his long stays at sea. But then Captain Thatch dismissed the help when the pirates' wives of Port Royal insisted it was their duty to look after the Widow Archer. Her house came to be known as Widow's Watch, and her hill, Widow's Reach.

Maxwell paused a moment to catch his breath halfway up Widow's Reach, and he looked up at the aging mansion that appeared much older than it was. Although the pirates' wives kept the inside of Widow's Watch maintained well enough, the outside—exposed to the heat of the sun, the wet of the rain, the often hostile winds—sustained damage that went mostly unattended.

There was someone else on the path: Maxwell caught a glimpse of a man making his way down and through an overgrown section of the steep incline. Jacob got off the trail and sat on a rock behind a bush to let the descending man pass in ignorance. This way Jacob wouldn't have to exchange amenities—something he wasn't in a mood to do. Jacob Maxwell believed a man should be left alone to climb Widow's Reach, taking the time it took in climbing the hill to collect himself before confronting the widow.

Discovering someone else on the path didn't surprise the captain of the *Bernadette*, with so many ships being in port; it was the practice of most captains to pay homage to the Widow Archer upon their ship's arrival. The captains—especially those who had been associated with Captain Thatch somehow—usually brought tributes.

Maxwell jumped to his feet when he saw it was Russell Gavette, his archenemy, that was coming down the trail.

Gavette caught Maxwell's sudden movement out of the corner of his eye, and reached for his saber. But Russell returned his half-drawn sword to its sheath after recognizing his archenemy, Jacob Maxwell, who was attempting to look as if he had been rudely inconvenienced.

Here was an awkward situation, like waking to unfamiliar surroundings. Revenge had been sworn by both against the other, but this was not the time or place for a fight: the two stood on Widow's Reach, and this was consecrated ground.

Maxwell and Gavette had once been best friends, growing up together on the streets of London and later fighting side by side on the high seas. There came a falling out shortly after Jacob became Captain Thatch's first mate. Maxwell often wondered if his promotion had something to do with the break. It certainly made reconciliation impossible.

A breach of faith had occurred—something that can never happen between partners. A best mate must, without reservation, lay down his life for his partner; an apparent hesitation on Russell Gavette's part brought an immediate dissolution of their friendship. In the heat of battle Russell had paused momentarily to evaluate whether Jacob needed assistance. Jacob interpreted the evaluation as a reluctance to join in the fight.

After the battle Russell had to leave the *Hargus,* of course, and he did so with an unspoken but well-understood desire to someday avenge the defamation of his character. Russell signed on with the *Rhinehart,* where he rapidly climbed the ranks to become her captain. He soon fashioned the *Rhinehart* into one of the better-respected privateers on the high seas.

Although it was inevitable the two captains would someday fight, a part of Jacob was still glad to see his former best mate standing before him on the trail, and he had to stop himself from inquiring after Russell's health. Jacob thought he could see in the eyes of his archenemy an urge to also say something—during the brief moment when their eyes met—before Russell realized the impossible situation and turned and continued down the path; and Jacob, too, put himself back to climbing.

No one answered Maxwell's knock after he arrived at the Watch; usually one or two pirates' wives were at the house when Jacob would come calling, but there didn't seem to be anyone around this time. With so many ships in port, the women were probably at home, busy being wives to their husbands.

The captain opened the large oak door himself, and lit a candle he found on the table in the foyer, and started looking around.

It was dark inside Widow's Watch. The windows were always heavily draped to keep out the scalding sun. Jacob entered the living room and shadows danced nervously across the walls, reacting to the flickering candle in his hand.

He found the Widow Archer in the study, where she nearly always sat, in the alcove of the bay window, in her rocking chair, rocking to and fro parallel to the window, slow and unremitting. Like the other drapes in the house, the bay window curtains remained closed, but here a single narrow gap ran from floor to ceiling, so if the widow's chair happened to be facing the window (which it never was), she would have a very limited view of Port Royal through the small opening.

The Widow Archer always looked straight ahead as if unaware of the window or the small opening between the drapes; but if anybody dared to change the position of the curtains or the chair, the old woman would fly into a rage.

"Greetings, Widow Archer," said Maxwell, carrying his candle into the gloomy study.

"We're all alone today, it seems." Jacob proceeded on over to a large oak desk in the corner of the room, to the desk once used by Captain Thatch to put his feet up. Jacob changed his mind about setting his candle down on the desk after getting a silly notion the flame would go out if he did. He shook his head to rid himself of the crazy idea, but he put the light down on a nearby lamp stand, anyway.

Jacob turned to the Widow Archer, still rocking in her chair, uninterrupted, as if the captain had never entered the room. Maxwell was always uneasy in the Watch, and being alone with the widow for the first time, he was stepping lighter than usual.

"I brought you a little something from Brest, France." Maxwell took a small silver powder box from his waistcoat and started to hand it to the widow but then stopped himself, remembering she never took anything directly from him or anybody else. He put the little box down next to the candle on the lamp stand.

"I lost my first mate at Brest," said the captain to the widow, who seemed as distant as the mountains on the moon. "I haven't decided on who to replace him with; it

57

ought to be Russell Gavette, a' course. The sour dog! Now with a ship of his own and a mind to pin my ears to the deck. The world twists and turns, does it not!"

When Maxwell would talk to the Widow Archer, it was like speaking to the ocean, the conversation always one-sided, his words emptying out into the unknown. But the Widow Archer had been known to speak; she was supposed to be able to see into the future, to tell fortunes. Captain Thatch had said he had used her advice on more than one occasion. But what kind of advice could that be? Jacob had been visiting the widow for more than three years and she had never said anything, had never *done* anything but rock in her chair.

"We finally got the cargo that should put the lads and myself up right handsomely—not that we're in need of loot, a' course, we've got plenty enough stashed away on our island to last us a while." Maxwell moved to the door as he spoke, and looked down the dark hallway to make sure he was alone. "Of course, that's if the lads would spend their shares more to the wise, which none of 'em ever seems to do. The reward we got for the Battle of Brest barely covered our expenses in The Hague."

Maxwell stopped his rambling.

Was the widow trying to speak?

Jacob returned to the rocking chair. The widow was mumbling something. He leaned over the old woman, and turned an ear to try to hear her words.

"Take heed, young captain," the Widow Archer was saying. "Take heed, young captain."

Suddenly, she stopped rocking, and reached out and grabbed Maxwell with an iron grip on his forearm, her fingernails digging into his skin.

"Ouch!" Maxwell tried to loose her hold, but she held fast. She pulled him closer, turning her somber face toward his. The widow looked at Jacob with deep, beseeching eyes.

> When is a queen not a queen
> And the red stone green?
> How can a man die twice
> And still not rest?

"See here, ma'am!" insisted Maxwell, trying again to unfasten her grip.

And then she did relax, with her muscles and her stare collapsing, the widow withdrew her fingernails and started rocking calmly again.

Maxwell backed away toward the study door. The old woman is clearly insane, he thought.

The lamp stand had tipped over and the candle was burning a hole in the carpet. Jacob came back to stamp out the fire, but then again hurried to be gone.

Look to the west
When the black heart beats no more.

The Widow Archer was speaking serenely now as she rocked, her voice seemed to come from a faraway place, one of contentment, as if she had found the solution to a quandary.

To find your prize,
Look to the west and the blacksmith's door.

"Crazy old woman!" Maxwell grumbled several times as he scrambled down the Reach, hurrying from the Watch, eager to rejoin his ship and the world of the sane.

chapter 5

THE DEAL

While Sheck Tilley was getting used to being a married man and while Captain Maxwell was paying his respects to the Widow Archer, Moon and Spike were busy pushing wheelbarrows along the myriad of planks and pilings that made up the large wharf of Port Royal. They were wheeling for the supply store, Pots and Pans, helping Emmett Sedgwick and his apprentice, Egan Shaw, replenish the ship's larder.

The proprietor of Pots and Pans, Ernest Munford, stood in the doorway of his dockside shop, watching the four *Bernadette* crewmen come his way. Munford was glad for the business, of course, but would it be enough?

Ernest Munford was in a bind. He needed money—a good deal of money—to pay for a shipment of New England furniture that was due any day. He had foolishly made himself cash poor by buying a large quantity of dry goods and perishables the week before, finding the low cost of the merchandise impossible to let pass without a bid.

Captain Ellis would no doubt take the furniture on down to South America if Munford didn't come up with the money, and the storekeeper would be out of the large down payment he had been obliged to make.

If only the arriving ships were buying up more goods! There had to be a reason the ships were coming to roost other than to resupply; they were certainly purchasing very little—not enough to replenish empty larders, anyway.

Munford pulled anxiously at the shoulder straps of his apron and bit deeply into the tobacco plug he was gnawing on. What was he going to do? Maybe the *Bernadette* is in need of a large purchase....

"Greetings, Mr. Munford," said young Egan Shaw, the first of the four *Bernadette* crewmen to arrive at Pots and Pans. He hurried past the storekeeper in the doorway to a jar of rock candy sitting on the counter inside. Close on Egan's heels were his three shipmates, also desiring the luxury of a sugar treat.

"So what will the good ship *Bernadette* be needing this time round?" inquired the smiling storekeeper, when he came back inside the store after spitting his chew into a spittoon on the boardwalk.

"Not much," said Emmett, between slurps of dissolving sugar, "mostly flour, a few pounds of bacon."

"Yes, well, we can certainly help you out there," Munford said, trying to suppress his anxiety regarding the furniture shipment.

Desperate situations require desperate measures; and so, after the wheelbarrows had been filled to Emmett's satisfaction, the storekeeper stepped behind his counter and beckoned the *Bernadette* lads to draw near. Munford took a deep breath and screwed his face into a look of serious concern, and after rolling his eyes as if considering whether he should be saying anything at all, he said, "Look, you fellas have been coming in here a long time, right? I feel about you like I do my own family. You know me and I know you. And that's why"—the shopkeeper leaned forward, with calculated enthusiasm—"I'm going to let you help me make us all rich!" He smiled broadly. "Have you ever heard of a fellow named Joshua Dobbs?"

The four *Bernadette* crewmen looked around at one another and shook their heads, no.

"He was a gunner on the *Rhinehart*, Russell Gavette's ship." Munford noticed the lads' eyebrows twitch with the mention of Gavette, their captain's rival. "He came in here one night just as I was closing shop, must've been about a month ago, drunk and getting drunker. He was pouring down rum from a bottle he was swinging, complaining bitterly about how the *Rhinehart* was going to ruin.

"Well, he went on about this and that, him and them—getting more drunk all the time—and asking me if I knew of any ship in need of a fine gunner such as himself."

Munford paused and looked behind his back at the storefront window to make sure no ears were pressing against the glass. Lowering his voice, he forced the *Bernadette* crewmen to lean forward to hear.

"And then Dobbs started talking about revenge, about how he knew where Gavette had buried his hoard, and about how he had a mind to collect it!

"Well, this was dangerous talk, I don't have to tell you!" Munford straightened back up and raised his voice once more. "The man was getting so drunk and angry. And then I don't know what came over me, but I kidded Dobbs about being too drunk to remember where Gavette's Island was—let alone his treasure.

"I was really sticking my neck out with that remark!" Sweat was forming on the storekeeper's brow, and he dabbed at it with his apron, for effect.

"So then Dobbs grabs a piece of wrapping paper that was lying on the counter here,"—Munford reached over and took a wrap from a stack at the end of the counter top—"and he starts scribbling and describing Gavette's Island like he'd been there just the day before."

Munford imitated the voice of the drunken pirate: "'Whadda-ya-thing-a-that,' said the fool, sticking the wrap in my face.

"But then Dobbs had a change of mind, his face turned pale, and he stepped back. He must have realized the foolish thing he had done!

"There he stood, swaying in his drunkenness like a sapling in a gale, trying to reason out what to do. You can believe I was sweating more than my share . . ." Munford again wiped some perspiration from his forehead. "Me, being a witness to his sacrilege against the *Rhinehart* and all!

"Well, he finally throws up his hands and lets out this crazy howl at the ceiling. And he tears up the map,"—Munford tore up the paper wrap he held—"and throws the pieces to the floor,"—Munford threw his—"and then he stomps out of my shop—just like that!"

The storekeeper paused a moment to catch his breath, before repeating: "Just like that!

"Next day, some lads from the *Rhinehart* came around looking for him, but Joshua Dobbs had just disappeared—nobody knows where. Probably fell off the slip and drowned in the shallows, and then drifted out with the tide. That's what I figure," said Ernest Munford, ending his story with a wink.

"Uh-hum," Spike cleared his throat, "and you still have

the map?"

Munford nodded his head to the affirmative, his face expressing true amazement.

Emmett joined in: "And now you want us to let Cap'n Maxwell know you'd be willing to part with the map—for a reasonable price, a' course?"

"Well . . ."

Before the storekeeper could further explain his position, the four *Bernadette* crewmen exploded with laugher.

"That's a right nice tale, Mr. Munford," said Egan, patting the storekeeper on the back with one hand and reaching into the jar of rock candy with the other.

"No! No! I don't want to sell it! I want to share . . ."

"I've heard a good many treasure map yarns," said Emmett, "and that's up there with the best of 'em, I suppose, but there was this one time . . ."

"No! No! Now listen, I'm telling you the truth, lads! Here, I've got it right here." Munford rummaged under the counter and came up with a crumpled, torn, and glued-back-together wrap. He had it folded over on itself so only a few scribbles could be seen; he didn't want to be giving the treasure away.

"We've seen treasure maps before," said Emmett, trying to sound unimpressed, but Munford could see a glint of curiosity in the old doctor-cook's eyes.

The storekeeper quickly returned the map to its hid-

ing place under the counter and came up with another
piece of paper. "I redid it so it's easier to read," he said,
again keeping the map mostly concealed so only an insignificant—but enticing—part of a sketch of an island was
visible.

"Whadda-ya-mean, you don't wanna sell it?" asked
Moon. All four privateers were now looking on with genu-
ine interest.

"I want just a share—a one in ten share, which seems
more than reasonable. And a holding fee, of course."

"Holding fee!" exclaimed Emmett. "What holding fee?"

"Oh, I don't know. Fifty pieces of eight ought to suffice—refundable, naturally, with the presentation of my
share."

The four *Bernadette* crewmen began talking all at once
but then settled down when Emmett raised his hand for
quiet. "You're saying we give you fifty in silver, go off and
do all the work of finding and digging up all our shares?
If you're so sure of the treasure, why do you need the fifty?"

The storekeeper said apologetically, "The *Bernadette* is
a fine ship, and her crew top-notch! But what if the Spanish or somebody else gets the better of you out there? Most
unlikely! But then if they take possession of our map? All
will be lost. And there is always the unfortunate storm at
sea. My friends, I will be giving you back the holding fee
upon your return—it is not as if you were taking a chance

of losing it. Of course not! If Joshua Dobbs proves to be a liar, and you don't find Gavette's stash, you are not out of anything. I will be returning the holding fee to you in any case."

"And it ain't like Mr. Munford here would be shippin' out with the holdings," added Moon, as he reached over the counter and patted the storekeeper soundly on the shoulder. "Like he's dumb enough to think there might be a place on Earth he could hide."

"My point exactly!" agreed Ernest Munford. "I am a friend, not a fool."

Emmett started for the door. "It would be up to the cap'n, and he's most likely to say no anyhow."

"He will come to see the advantage of the proposal, as you lads have. I'm sure of it," replied Munford, cheerfully seeing the men out of his store. "Tell Captain Maxwell to come and see me so I can better explain our good fortune in obtaining the map."

From the doorway the storekeeper watched the buccaneers wheel their supplies back down the wharf to the *Bernadette*'s longboat. Munford couldn't restrain himself from rubbing his hands together, his troubles being nearly over. He was sure Maxwell's men would convince their captain to accept the deal. The storekeeper would have the money for the fine New England furniture after all. Several pirates' wives were already waiting for the delivery. He would use the holding fee to pay for the furniture and earn it back in plenty of time to give to the disappointed *Bernadette* lads upon their return. Perhaps he would offer a special price to the *Bernadette* on her next order of supplies. Yes, indeed, that was the least he could do for his friends.

"Absolutely not!" roared Captain Maxwell, when Emmett suggested Munford's deal. "Of all things, how could you be taken in by a treasure map ruse! We don't have fifty in silver anyhow."

"Actually we do," said Quartermaster Fenton, who was with the captain when the four presented themselves back on board, "but just barely."

"No!" said the captain emphatically. "We have to get the Lady Howard to England as soon as we can. We don't have time for this tomfoolery!" Maxwell was in a bad mood, owing to his unpleasant visit with the widow.

"And I've changed my mind about sailing in the morning," added the captain. "We're leaving port tonight—before anything goes wrong. I've got a bad feeling."

"But we can't leave now, Cap'n," said Spike. "All the lads are ashore and won't be back till morning."

"This deal with Munford, I don't see how it could be a swindle," insisted Emmett.

"There's no way we'd be losin' any money," added Moon.

"No, I said!" said Maxwell. "Not with the ship's swag,

you don't. Use your own fool money if you want to throw your shares away, but the *Bernadette*'s silver stays put—what's left of it, that is."

This gave Emmett an idea. "Why don't we use our own shares, lads? We certainly have plenty among us."

"But it's on Rum Cay," said Spike.

Rum Cay, or Maxwell's Island, was where the *Bernadette* crew kept their hoard buried for safekeeping. Every privateer or pirate ship had an island in the Caribbean where her crew stashed their accumulation of loot.

"We have to go by Rum Cay, anyway, before we head back to Europe, ain't that so, Cap'n?" said Emmett. "We can use what's on the *Bernadette* now, and then replace it with our shares once we get to Rum Cay."

Maxwell's face twisted into a scowl as he was unable to think of an argument to convincingly dismiss the proposal. "I don't like it! Do as ya please, but we're still leaving port tonight! Spike, Moon, come with me. We're gonna round up the lads."

* * *

Moon plopped a sack of fifty silver pieces of eight down on the Pots and Pans' counter in front of Ernest Munford. And then he took the map of Gavette's Island from the storekeeper, and stuffed it in his shirt without looking at it—keeping Maxwell from getting a peek.

"What is this!" laughed Maxwell.

"Since you ain't in on the deal," said Moon.

"But I'm your dear captain!" Maxwell playfully tried to reach into Moon's shirt for the map. Moon spun away with a growl.

Maxwell growled back. And there they stood, crouched down, nose to nose, growling at each other like two mad dogs. Then, with a wink from the captain, they both exploded with laughter, along with Spike. Ernest Munford breathed a sigh of relief; he had feared that his store was about to come tumbling down around him in the heat of a battle.

"Glad to see you back with the incurable, Cap'n," said Spike. "You were carrying on something serious. Was it the Widow Archer again?" Maxwell had complained before about his required visits to the Watch.

"Oh, the dear saintly woman," Maxwell thickened his cockney accent. "We had a spot a' tea in the garden and then we all played a bit a' croquet on the lawn. . . . We let 'Er 'Ighness win, a' course."

"A' course!" said Spike, in his best cockney.

"A' course!" followed Moon.

The three members of the *Bernadette* then looked meaningfully at Ernest Munford.

"A' course! A' course!" The storekeeper joined in.

"So, do we still have to sail tonight?" Moon asked his captain.

"I've got a bad feeling," Maxwell said, serious again. He walked to the door for a look around. The night was fast approaching. "Who is this?" On the other side of the boardwalk, two figures in the long afternoon shadow of a shack moved quickly to the nearest alley when Maxwell looked their way. "I think it best we sail."

But at Barnacle Bob's, where Maxwell first tried to collect some of his men, he came to realize—after a lengthy exchange of opinions with some members of his crew and with Bob, who kept plying him with free drink and reason—that it would take the rest of the night to find everybody, so why waste the time and effort if the *Bernadette* would be sailing in the morning, anyway?

Maxwell was persuaded but still not convinced the *Bernadette* shouldn't sail at once. He was standing uneasily at the bar, finishing his last drink, when Cory Heath and Zak Drago entered the tavern and told him about two odd characters requesting a parley with him outside.

"How do you mean, 'odd'?" asked Maxwell.

"Like in weasels and shadow stealers," said Cory.

"Like in creepy, slitherin' snakes," suggested Zak.

Intrigued, Maxwell followed Zak and Cory outside. It was early evening. Main Street was busy with the clamor of buccaneers at play. The alley adjacent to Barnacle Bob's was in shadows; Maxwell came to a stop after taking a few cautious steps into the dead end.

"Down here, Captain Maxwell," said a low voice.

"You wanna see me? Then step up and show yourselves." Maxwell stood tall in the middle of the alley with his hands on his hips. Zak and Cory took their places on either side of their captain.

Two men, that Maxwell recognized as those he had seen scurrying away earlier into an alley near Pots and Pans, stepped out of the shadows. One of them, carrying a small box, dragged himself from the darkest corner of the alley as if he feared the moonlight would burn his delicate complexion.

"Razmus Foote," said he, cradling the wooden box like a baby in his arms. "And this is the honorable Frederick Sparano."

Sparano removed a narrow-rimmed Portuguese hat from his head, and bowed. "Proud to make your acquaintance, Captain Maxwell. Your reputation precedes you."

"Whatever one that might be," said Maxwell. Sparano's movements were smooth, like his voice, and confident, most likely the product of some fancy school. Sparano's sword and sheath dangled naturally at his side. Maxwell knew that he had just been introduced to a man who would never seriously bow to anyone.

The overtly polite Razmus Foote favored the right side

of his face, keeping it aslant—turned slightly down and away. Maxwell had seen the mannerism before; it belonged to the unfortunate one caught and branded for the crime of theft, the letter T burned into the cheek. Most who bore the stigma wore it proudly while in the company of fellow buccaneers. Or they ignored the injury. Only those who held jealously to their innocence, or those who were ashamed of their mistakes, felt a need to hide the mark.

"We understand the *Bernadette* is sailing for Alberton in the morning?" inquired Razmus Foote.

This is what the *Bernadette* crew had been told to say if asked.

"What of it?" replied Maxwell.

"Mr. Sparano and I have urgent business in Alberton. We would greatly appreciate the transport, and we would reward you generously for your kindness." Foote swayed rhythmically as he spoke, like a blade of grass in a breeze, maybe a little drunk. He stroked the box he was carrying as if it were a cat.

"Well, now, I'd truly like to accommodate you gentlemen. But it turns out the *Bernadette* will have to be layin' over here in Port Royal a few days, and then we'll be headin' on down to Maracaibo; a change of plan—business, ya know. Have you inquired about the *Bristol?* I hear she's headin' for Alberton."

"Unfortunate, unfortunate indeed," mumbled Razmus

Foote, picking at his little wooden box absentmindedly with a fingernail. "The *Bristol*: now there is a fine ship, too. Is it not, Mr. Sparano? Yes, thank you, Captain. Perhaps another time."

Foote made an about-face and hurried off. His henchmen, Frederick Sparano, performed another elegant bow before departing.

"Now, how would you like to haul a boatload of them snakes to market," said Maxwell, after the two denizens of the night had slithered back into the shadows.

"What do you suppose was in the box?" Zak wondered.

"Somebody's head, no doubt," said Cory.

"I'm going back to the ship," said Maxwell. "I've got a bad feeling."

* * *

Rebecca Webb opened the captain's cabin door to the captain. "Come in, sir," she said.

Maxwell had knocked on the ladies' door the first thing after coming back aboard; he wanted to make sure the royal cargo was still safe. "You're keeping yourselves away from the port'oles? We can't let on you're here."

"Of course, Captain Maxwell," said Sarah. "We have been as quiet as mice and as bored as nails! Oh, how I'd love to go ashore! I've never been to the Caribbean."

"At Rum Cay you can have a good walk about, but until then we have to keep you a secret."

Rebecca asked, "Is everything all right, Captain? You look worried."

"Fine, fine. I'll just be glad to be under way is all. There's too many ships in port—too many things that can go wrong. But everything is as it should be. Have a good night, ladies. We'll be off first thing in the morning."

Maxwell doubled the watch before going below. And he returned to the deck three times before finally climbing into his hammock in the crew's quarters.

chapter 6

THE RIDDLE

Sheck Tilley spoke softly, "Captain Maxwell?" He pulled at his captain's shirtsleeve to gently wake him. It was still dark. A night candle—the wick of which was threatening to drown in its own wax—flickered in a small tin lantern hanging from an exposed rib in the ship's inner hull. The weak flame was the only light in the cavernous sleeping quarters that had once been the main cargo hold of the *Bernadette*, before she became a privateer. A wide variety of berths were built into the sleeping quarters, reflecting the many tastes of the crewmen who had made them: from well-furnished cabins with doors and feather mattresses on their bunks, to a mere blanket heaped in a pile against the bulkhead to reserve a shipmate's resting place.

"What is it?" Maxwell yawned, rubbing his eyes, struggling to sit up in his precarious rope hammock.

Sheck Tilley informed his captain, "I've just come aboard and there's nobody on deck."

"What!" Maxwell nearly hung himself in the hammock as he tried to jump to his feet.

Kipp Rafferty helped Sheck untangle the captain, and then they all ran for the aft hatch ladder.

The stars in the eastern sky were beginning to fade as Maxwell and his men arrived topside. Maxwell ran across the main deck and pounded on the door of the captain's cabin. Getting no response, he lifted the latch and the door swung open—it should have been locked!

The captain and his men froze in disbelief. A rude silence rushed from the vacant cabin like a bad smell. Maxwell felt like screaming, shouting an order. But what? He crossed the deck and grabbed hold of the ship's rail to steady himself, his eyes sweeping the deceptively quiet quay and shantytown along the shore.

Ivy Sabin had, by now, reached the crow's nest, and was beginning to scan the horizon with his spyglass.

"Blast!" Maxwell slammed his fist down on the rail. "Anything?" he shouted up at Ivy.

"Not yet."

Quartermaster Fenton, oil lamp in hand, nightcap still on his head, reported to the captain, "Dugan and Harper are missing."

Dugan and Harper had the night watch.

"The worthless beggars!" the captain cursed.

"Ahoy, canvas to the north," Ivy announced. "And headed north."

"Weigh anchor, lads!" ordered the captain. Maxwell surveyed the harbor to determine which vessel had left. "That berth there," he said, pointing at an empty mooring between two ships where he remembered a galleon had sat the day before. "What ship was that?"

"The *Catlow*," said Emmett.

"Aye! Vernon Tate's galleon," added Moon.

The *Bernadette* eased her way out of the harbor, again skirting the two death cages secured to the coral reef. Inside each cage a head bobbed face down in the ship's wake.

"Good riddance!" Kipp mumbled, joining the captain at the rail.

Something didn't look right, the pattern of Haylock's shirt?

"That's odd," said the captain, before shouting an order to: "Heave to! Drop anchor and lower a bumboat!" He turned to Kipp. "You and Sheck go back and have a look at Haylock's mug. I don't believe that's him."

After rowing back to Haylock's watery prison, Kipp stuck the end of his oar between the bars of the cage and lifted up the face of—Gus Rockwood!

"What's *he* doin' in there!" exclaimed Kipp and Sheck together. They had just seen the drunken lout the day before, carousing in the streets of Port Royal.

* * *

The morning came and went without a decent breeze. Maxwell paced impatiently back and forth to while away a stagnant afternoon; little wind and no word from his lookout, no further sign of the sails Ivy had seen earlier. The Catlow had gotten too good a start on the *Bernadette*. Would she head west or steer east to try to lose herself? Or would she continue north for the Gulf Stream? "Damn!" If only the *Bernadette* had sailed the night before. How had Maxwell let his men talk him out of it! He felt like busting some heads, his own included.

The men were respecting Maxwell's displeasure by giving their captain a wide berth. The long day dragged on with barely a breeze flirting with the *Bernadette*'s sails, and then the wind stopped altogether with the coming of twilight.

Earlier in the day, Quartermaster Harley Fenton had found an irregularity in ship operations. It was his duty to inform the captain, but Harley was withholding the seemingly unimportant particular to avoid the captain's foul mood. When Harley finally did address his captain, he was the first man to speak to Maxwell that day, and it was now almost night.

"Captain Maxwell, it appears some stores were broken into last night," Harley reported.

"What!" roared the captain, trying to think of an excuse to box Fenton's ears.

"Over here, Cap'n." The quartermaster led Maxwell to some sacks of flour and a barrel of salt pork that had been purchased the day before at Pots and Pans. The supplies rested up against the forecastle between the forward hatch and starboard scuppers. One of the sacks was untied and spilling flour. The barrel's lid was ajar.

"Where's the cook? Why wasn't this stowed away?"

"It was probably one of them kidnappers," Emmett suggested, attempting to distract attention from his lapse in responsibility. Both Emmett and Egan had gotten careless with the supplies after bringing them aboard, being caught up with the business concerning the treasure map at the time. "The scoundrels probably looked to see if there was anything worth taking, and then let it go, seeing it was just a bit of flour and bacon."

"A small matter, is it? My dear cook! Kind benefactor of birds and rats! If you find food so trivial a matter, why don't we all go without supper tonight!" Maxwell was feeling better now, having vented some of his frustration.

It was late when Maxwell retired to his cabin for the

night, and found it hard to fall asleep. He had his cabin back, and his large mahogany bed, but the scent of Sarah's and Rebecca's perfumes haunted the room; many of the ladies' belongings were still laying about here and there. Maxwell had been fuming all day about the diminished prospects of obtaining a queen's commission, and for having to chase after the *Catlow* like he did the *De la Cruz* all those long days across the endless Atlantic. . . . But as the captain tossed fitfully under his covers this night, a touch of guilt was also bedeviling him. Lady Howard had been his guest, so to speak, so mightn't he also be considered at least partly responsible for her disappearance?

Maxwell awoke to what he thought was Sheck Tilley shaking his hammock again, but it was a rough sea that was rocking his bed and pounding the ship.

The captain growled when he came on deck to find he had overslept. It was well into morning. The ocean was heavy and spray shot over the *Bernadette*'s bow as she slammed into a large swell. The skies were gray and a light rain swirled in a buffeting wind. But the *Bernadette* had made good time while her captain slept, nearly completing the Windward Passage. Looking to starboard, Maxwell saw that his ship lay between Cape St. Nick and Tortuga Island, northwest of Haiti. Soon the ship would be entering the Gulf Stream and sailing up the lee side of Cuba.

Brice Depwig was at the wheel.

"Report, helmsman."

"A bit of weather, sir, but steady enough," said Depwig.

Maxwell returned to his cabin to put on his sealskins; his men were already wearing their rain gear to keep off the drizzle; it was seldom cold at these latitudes, but the wet was always a bother.

In a few hours the *Bernadette* was riding the Gulf Stream, sailing at a good clip despite having to beat into a wind. But was she headed in the right direction? Maxwell hoped the same luck that had led him to the *De la Cruz* would now help him find the *Catlow*.

The men were keeping to themselves; foul weather encourages solitude; standing next to someone is awkward on the slippery deck of a yawing ship.

The rest of the morning was active, with the rigging having to be adjusted for a number of tacks.

And then Link Spivey happened upon Shell Haylock stowing away in a forward locker of the *Bernadette*'s forecastle!

Haylock wrestled Spivey's sword away from him in a short scuffle where Spivey first screamed as though he'd uncovered the devil himself and then took off running for his life with the Lord of Pitchforks on his heels!

Maxwell was on the quarterdeck, looking forward, when Spivey and Haylock came flying at him out of the forecastle. Spivey slipped and fell on the wet deck as the ship lurched suddenly in the heavy seas, and Haylock tumbled over Spivey.

Haylock pulled himself to his feet and squinted at his surroundings; his eyes needed focusing after being so long in the dark forward locker. He brandished Spivey's sword, taking slices out of the empty air around him, warding off possible attackers. But nobody made a move in his direction. Everybody just stood and stared at Haylock, dumbfounded.

Haylock pulled at his long, tangled mane, trying to think. Spivey had roused him from a deep sleep, the first sleep he had had in days. Haylock was disoriented and half-mad from his ordeal in the cage. What hell was he in now? Was it the ship that was gyrating, or was it his mind?

Maxwell was impressed. Shell Haylock! Staggering around amidships the *Bernadette!* Haylock, then, had elected to swim for the *Bernadette* after his escape from his cage—instead of making for the unfriendly shores of Jamaica. And it was he who had gotten into the flour and salt pork; there were flour smears at the corners of the devil's mouth, looking like drool on the jaws of a mad dog. There were also white smudges on his tattered clothing, on his hands, and in his matted hair.

After a long moment, the crew recovered from the shock of Haylock's sudden appearance and began to cautiously sidle up to the scoundrel, swords drawn, taking heed of the precarious footing on the wavering, slippery deck.

"Here, good friends! No need to go to all this trouble on my account!" Haylock declared. But as he looked into the steely, determined eyes of the encircling privateers, it was obvious that reason would not stand him in good stead. With a leap he was on the rail at the main-shroud, and he started climbing the rope lattice for the crow's nest, where Ivy Sabin sat ready to club him with his spyglass once he arrived. Haylock was near the nest when Maxwell shouted an order that stopped both Haylock and the crewmen who had followed him up the shroud.

"Hold on there, lads!

"Mr. Haylock, suppose you explain how you come to be on my ship!"

"Good day, Cap'n!" Haylock shouted down to Maxwell on the quarterdeck. "That would be an amazing tale, worthy of a spot of grog and a seat at your fine table, I dare say—if you would be so kind as to allow me safe passage." Haylock started down the main-shroud but was interrupted by a sudden pitch of the ship, causing him to almost lose his hold.

"What became of Gus Rockwood?" demanded Kipp Rafferty, on the shroud at Haylock's feet.

"Gus Rockwood? Sorry, but I never had the pleasure, friend."

"He was the bloke we found in your cage," said Kipp.

"Oh yes, that kind gentleman! Well, now, he came to help me out of my unfortunate circumstance, he did. Slipped and hit his poor head against my terrible cage, then, if I recall. Aye, tragic it was."

"You mean he fell for your promise of gold, and then you did a switch on 'em!" accused Kipp.

"I assure ye . . ."

"Haylock!" shouted the captain. "Did you have any business with a certain party we were transporting?"

"Well, now, you'd be referrin' to more than one party, wouldn't ye, sir? Two is more the count, I'd say. Yes, indeed! I seen the affair as I was comin' aboard, I did. Seen them two hauled away in gunnies, I did. I never seen them that was all tied up. No, sir. But I seen them who was doin' the haulin'! I surely did that, Cap'n!"

Haylock smiled a devilish grin, believing he might live yet! He would trade his neck for what he had seen— maybe even get more out of the exchange . . . if he could just get his muddled brain to behave . . . if he could just clear out some of the stubborn cobwebs. It didn't help being swung about high on the main-mast of a tall ship in the grips of foul weather.

"Let 'em down," ordered Maxwell.

Shell Haylock descended the main-shroud too eagerly in his happiness at being given a hearing, not paying proper attention to the rough waters. The *Bernadette* lurched and the poor devil lost his hold again, and for good. Haylock so despised himself for the stupid blunder that he refused to register a complaint as he fell, headfirst, to the hard deck below.

Moon approached the still, twisted body of Shell Haylock, and gave it a nudge with the toe of his boot.

"Ain't that the way of the world!" Moon complained. "There actually comes a time when Haylock's miserable life is worth a damn, and he up and gets hisself killed! The black heart!"

"What did you say?" asked Maxwell, coming up beside Moon.

"Just that the beggar is finally worth more alive than dead, and what does he do?"

"About his heart? You said he had a 'black heart'?"

"Aye, a black heart. If ever there was."

Maxwell rubbed his left forearm where the Widow Archer had grasped him so tightly.

"Hard aport, helmsman!" The captain hurried to the port rail and began searching the gray mist and angry waters. "Due west, lads, and keep 'er steady!"

He shouted to his lookout, "Ivy, you keep a sharp eye up there!

"Bos'n! Look to your duties!" Maxwell yelled at Wesley Tuttle, his boatswain, who was staring at his captain as if unsure he had heard him correctly; but then Wesley jumped to and began shouting orders of his own, to trim the sails for a proper tack west.

"Emmett, come with me!" Maxwell shouted, and headed for his cabin.

Emmett Sedgwick, the ship's surgeon and cook, hurried after his captain. And following Emmett, as always, his apprentice, young Egan Shaw.

Once inside, Maxwell started pacing back and forth, still clasping his forearm as if to keep it from bleeding. Emmett and Egan took seats at the captain's table.

Maxwell explained, "I'm sure you've heard all the crazy stories about how the Widow Archer was supposed to be some kind of fortune teller, warning against evils and storms and bad business practices. And you know I think it's all a bunch of malarkey."

Maxwell pulled off his sealskin jacket and tossed it on the bed. "Well, when I was up there, this last time, she gave me some words." The captain stopped pacing and sat down at the table with Emmett and Egan, and ran his fingers through his hair.

"Go on, what'd she say?" implored Emmett. "I ain't never dismissed the Widow Archer, and Cap'n Thatch never did neither."

"I know. I didn't even think about what she said, till Haylock falls on his fool head just now, and Moon reminds me." Maxwell recalled the widow's words, etched deep in his memory along with the feel of her iron grip on his arm:

> When is a queen not a queen
> And the red stone green?
> How can a man die twice
> And still not rest?
>
> Look to the west
> When the black heart beats no more.
> To find your prize,
> Look to the west and the blacksmith's door.

Emmett took out his pipe and put a match to it. "That part about the black heart and going west is the reason we're headed that way now?"

"Aye! When Moon said Haylock had a black heart, that's when I remembered what the widow said."

"I was wondering why you had us change course, running us straight for Cuba."

Cuba was Spain's stronghold in the Caribbean, and the major stopover for Spanish ships returning to Europe from the New World. The Gulf Stream flowed by Cuba and was used by most ships heading north and east, and not just Spanish vessels. But it was wise for pirates to steer clear of Cuba, and now the *Bernadette* was heading straight for Havana, the most heavily fortified port in Cuba if not the entire Spanish Empire!

"And where it goes, 'How can a man die twice / And still not rest?'," Emmett continued, "is referring to Haylock again. We took Haylock for dead in his cage, and then he dies once more on the deck just now. We still have unfinished business with Mr. Haylock, and that goes with the 'not resting' part of the riddle." Emmett drew deeply on his pipe and blew out a long curl of smoke. "But when is a queen not a queen?"

"Do you think Queen Elizabeth is an impostor?" asked young Egan.

"Highly unlikely," said Emmett, suppressing a smile.

"How's about when a queen ain't doing her duties, when she don't act like a queen should be acting?" speculated Maxwell.

The three sat quietly pondering the possibilities for a moment, until there came a knock on the door. It was Toby Gant.

"Ivy spotted some canvas, Cap'n."

A galleon was three points aport the bow and heading north when Maxwell took his place on the quarterdeck.

"Bring 'er near, lads!"

The wind and waves were beginning to settle, and a partial silhouette of Cuba's coastline appeared ominously in the mist as the *Bernadette* drew near enough to the unknown vessel so it could be identified by Ivy.

"There flies the *Mary Ann*, Cap'n," shouted the *Bernadette*'s lookout.

Maxwell remembered the *Mary Ann* being anchored at Port Royal when the *Bernadette* had left that harbor. She must have departed shortly after the *Bernadette*. Had Sarah Howard been aboard the *Mary Ann* all along? This was easy! Maxwell would have to take an extra tribute to the Widow Archer on his next visit to the Watch.

"A queen is not a queen when she is a ship!" exclaimed Emmett. "The *Mary Ann* is named for the devout Queen Mary the Second."

* * *

The captain of the *Mary Ann*, Billy Beaumont, raised a white parley flag in a hurry after Maxwell fired a shot across his ship's bow. The *Mary Ann* was a fine ship, carrying a better crew than most, and would have put up a good fight on Beaumont's order. But a battle wasn't necessary because the captain of the *Mary Ann* knew Jacob Maxwell and the superior capabilities of the *Bernadette*. And Billy Beaumont had sailed on the *Hargus*, a few years alongside Jacob Maxwell, and considered Maxwell an acquaintance if not a friend.

Maxwell and eight of his crew rowed over to the *Mary*

Ann in the *Bernadette*'s longboat.

"Good afternoon, Captain," said Billy Beaumont, welcoming Maxwell and his men aboard. "What matter of business brings you to the *Mary Ann*?"

"Lady Sarah Howard!" Maxwell shot back, point blank, and boldly—considering the *Bernadette*'s captain and crew were standing outnumbered on the deck of somebody else's ship. But Maxwell wanted Billy Beaumont and his men to know his confidence: the *Bernadette* would make short work of the *Mary Ann* if necessary. "We have reason to believe Lady Howard is aboard your ship."

Captain Beaumont grew wide-eyed. "Excuse me, Cap'n, but I have no idea . . ."

"Then you'll have no problem with us taking a look around, now would ye." Maxwell nodded to his men, who scattered to make a search.

"Might I offer you a spot a' rum?" suggested the imposed-upon captain, saltily, bowing and sweeping his arm in an exaggerated motion in the direction of his cabin.

Maxwell accepted, half-expecting to find Sarah Howard upon entering the cabin. When offered a chair at Beaumont's table, Maxwell declined, preferring to stand by the door he had left open, believing that at any moment he would be hearing the shout of one of his men discovering the women.

When the announcement was not forthcoming, Maxwell began to have doubts, could he have been mistaken? Maybe it wasn't the *Mary Ann* the riddle was referring to. Perhaps the correct destination lay farther west. Somewhere on Cuba? Or had the widow been wrong all the way around? Was the business with Shell Haylock just a coincidence?

Maxwell accepted Billy Beaumont's offer of another swallow of rum. And he was just about to take a seat at his friend's table, and apologize for his rude behavior . . .

"Captain?" Kipp Rafferty was at the door with Sheck Tilley.

Maxwell growled, "What is it?" Kipp and Sheck didn't have the air of men finding what they had been told to find.

"No sign of Her Ladyship, Cap'n, but we did make an interesting discovery."

The two men led their captain to Morris Biggs of the *Catlow*, who was trying to blend into a group of Beaumont's men, and doing a poor job of it.

Fidgeting nervously when Kipp first spied him, Biggs became even more jittery with the approach of the imposing captain of the *Bernadette*, appearing to be in a mood to wring somebody's neck!

"Morris Biggs of the *Catlow*, Cap'n," said Kipp, as he and Sheck grabbed the nervous Biggs and pulled him from the circle of Beaumont's men.

"Aye! I recognize the mug! What brings you to the *Mary Ann*, Morris Biggs?" Maxwell put a serious face into that of the frightened pirate, whose eyes were begging Billy Beaumont for rescue.

"He came aboard yesterday morning," said Captain Beaumont, "telling us about the unfortunate kidnapping of the Lady Howard. We were just now on our way to see if we could . . ."

"In his own words!" interrupted Maxwell. "Tell us your tale, Biggs!"

"Like Cap'n Beaumont was sayin', they brings the lady aboard, and then I swims for the *Mary Ann* for help."

"To make a deal of your own is more how it was!" said Maxwell, growing red in the face. "Who was it brought the lady aboard the *Catlow*? I lost two good mates on account of them scoundrels, so don't ire me!"

"One of 'em called the other Mr. Sparrow."

"Sparano! Frederick Sparano?"

"Aye, Cap'n, that's him!" Morris Biggs relaxed a little, relieved that Maxwell knew of the man. "They made a deal with Cap'n Tate."

"Where are they headed?"

"I heard 'em mention Nassau."

"Whereabouts in Nassau?"

"I don't know! Honest, Cap'n!"

Maxwell growled, "You wouldn't happen to be a blacksmith, would ye?"

"Who, me? No, sir. I don't like horses."

"Know any blacksmiths in Nassau?"

Biggs tried to think. "Atkin's Harnesses?"

Maxwell shouted so all could hear, "Is there a black-smith on board?" Few ships besides whalers included a blacksmith among their crew. After no one aboard the *Mary Ann* admitted to being one, Maxwell said, "How about you, Cap'n Beaumont, you know any smithies in Nassau? I've got some buckle-work needs done."

"There's the Ready Anvil and Hot Iron." And Billy's men mentioned some others.

Maxwell took Beaumont aside. "I'm going to have to relieve the *Mary Ann* of her canvas, of course. We don't require any assistance in rescuing the Lady Howard, if you catch my drift. I could do worse and you know the facts. But you're a friend and sail an honest ship, and I don't hold nothin' against ye."

"Every ship that was in Port Royal will be giving the *Bernadette* chase," said Captain Beaumont. "They still think you hold Lady Howard."

Maxwell shook his head. "No, that don't surprise me much."

* * *

The *Bernadette* continued on for Nassau after her crew had stripped the *Mary Ann* of her sails—all the sails but those on her mainmast, leaving the *Mary Ann* enough canvas to make, at a slow pace, the next friendly port.

The skies further cleared and a modest breeze changed direction to help push the *Bernadette* along the Gulf Steam, but Ivy didn't see the *Catlow*'s or any other ship's sails the rest of the day.

Moon and Spike called on Maxwell in his cabin that night.

Moon laid the map of Gavette's Island and one of the Caribbean out on the captain's table. "Look at this, Cap'n," said Moon, pointing out locations on the maps. "This here is the end of the Man of War Channel, and that would make Gavette's Island one of the Jumento Cays, here."

"We could stop on our way to New Providence, Cap'n," added Spike. "Be on and off with the treasure in no time."

"We don't have no time, Spike. What we have is every ship in the world at our backs, thinking we still carry Lady Howard. We've got to find the *Catlow* before *we* go down."

"Nobody but the *Mary Ann* knows we're headed for Nassau, and she'll be keeping the information to herself," said Moon.

"Aye, but Nassau is one of the first places the dogs will look."

Nassau was the last stopover for pirate ships on their

way to Bermuda, Europe, or the North American colonies.

"Then how about dropping us off?" suggested Spike, with Moon nodding his approval of the idea.

"Who? You and Moon, Emmett and Egan? I'll be needing the lot of you if there is fighting to be done—which is most likely."

"How's about just me and Moon, then," said Spike. "The *Bernadette* can manage fine without the likes of us for a few days."

"But it might be weeks or even months before we return. What if the *Bernadette* goes down? You'll be marooned."

Spike and Moon laughed. And Spike said, "If it were a fleet of Spanish warships you was goin' up against, I should be concerned. But you're facin' nothin' but scalawags. However, if it would ease your mind, you can lend us the use of the longboat."

Ivy spotted the first of the Jumento Cays early the next morning. Moon and Spike were let down to sea in the longboat and were fast away with two weeks' supply of food and water. Jacob Maxwell begrudgingly watched them depart; he didn't like the idea of sailing on without his two best soldiers, but he owed them this request if not more; Moon and Spike had served him well, and if this venture was important to them, then so be it. And who knows, maybe one of the Jumento Cays *is* Gavette's Island; Moon and Spike can come away with a fortune.

But if they do, and Emmett and Egan share in the wealth, why would any of them bother to continue on in the service of Maxwell? They would most likely purchase their own vessel, or retire! Maxwell was in a foul mood again the rest of the day.

Before sunrise the next morning, the *Bernadette* was off Delaport Point, New Providence Island. The captain took a handful of men and two bumboats ashore. The ship continued on to the desert island of Rum Cay to replenish her dwindling swag of gold and silver, and to keep out of sight. She was to return to Delaport Point in two days to pick up Maxwell and his men and, if the winds blew fair, the Lady Howard.

chapter 7

GAVETTE'S
ISLAND

Have you thought about what you might do with your share of the treasure, Moon?" inquired Spike. He and Moon had just hauled the *Bernadette*'s longboat up the narrow, sandy shore of a little island in the Jumento Cays.

"I haven't thought about it, and you shouldn't either! You know it's bad luck!"

After unstepping the mast of the skiff, they walked the beach, searching the dense green jungle for a path inland.

This was the first island worthy of the name the two buccaneers had come upon since departing the *Bernadette* several hours earlier. The cays before this one had been no more than small sandbanks crowning low, uninviting coral reefs.

Spike and Moon gathered some brush and palm fronds to conceal the longboat before they ventured into the pathless jungle. They needed to view the island from a high point and compare it with the map, so they headed for the larger of a few hills in the north. The going was slow through the thick, steaming hot jungle that was swarming with bugs of all kinds.

"Pooh!" Spike spit out an insect that had flown into his mouth. "Are you sure we haven't been going around in circles? Seems like we've been at it for hours!"

It had actually been less than half an hour.

Moon came to a halt. "You take the lead, then."

They paused a moment to catch their breath. The annoying buzz of countless insects surrounded them, giving voice to the suffocating jungle. An occasional call of a bird in the distance was heard, suggesting to Spike a signal to retreat. Spike was having second thoughts about his and Moon's departure from the *Bernadette*.

"Maybe we should've stuck with the cap'n, Moon, till the business with Lady Howard was done, and then gone after Gavette's gold."

Moon was also feeling guilty about leaving Captain Maxwell and the others to deal with the kidnapping without the benefit of Spike and himself, but he would never mention the notion to anybody, even to his little Irish friend. "What? Don't be daft! The cap'n and the lads will make short work of Tate and the *Catlow*, and be back here in no time, for us and the treasure."

"You're right, mate," agreed Spike, feeling better for having voiced his concern. He unsheathed his saber and started hacking away at the underbrush.

They soon came to the base of a hill and started slogging their way up the slope. And after a while that seemed like forever, Moon and Spike finally stood—huffing and puffing—atop the highest hill on the little island.

The first thing they noticed was that they could have saved themselves a lot of trouble by continuing on in the longboat around the island. There was a large lagoon in the southeast and a creek bed wending its way down to it from the hills. The creek was dry from lack of rain, and they could have used it to gain access to the hills rather than beating a path the hard way up the west side of the island.

Moon removed the treasure map from his sweat-soaked shirt; and, using a compass, laid it out on the ground, north to south.

The island on the map showed two large lagoons, a forking river running west to east, a set of high peaks, and a rocky cliff. It was more of a rectangle than the little round cay the two *Bernadette* crewmen found themselves on.

"We've been had," said Moon.

"Maybe it's one of those, farther east," said Spike, pointing to more islands in the distance, spots of green on the blue sea.

"Oh, bother!" exclaimed a disappointed Moon. He sprawled out on the ground in the checkered shade of a little hardwood tree to take a nap.

"Look at that," said Spike, still scanning the water. "Some sails in the west."

Moon wasn't interested and was soon snoring away like a bear in winter.

Spike watched the vessel approach, and then kicked Moon awake when the ship started circling the island. It was the *Rhinehart*, Russell Gavette's galleon!

A pirate ship typically circumnavigated her island at least once before dropping anchor, to make sure nobody else was about. Moon and Spike bit their knuckles as the *Rhinehart* came around to where the *Bernadette*'s foliage-draped longboat sat on the beach like a wart on the hand of a beautiful woman. But the camouflage apparently did its job, because Gavette's ship continued on without hesitating, circling the island till it came to the lagoon in the southeast, where she then struck sail.

Moon and Spike descended the hill as fast as they could through the unobliging jungle, arriving at the lagoon just in time to see a load of pirates spill out of a longboat onto the beach.

To the amazement of the two *Bernadette* crewmen,

Armand Delcarpio walked up the sand with Russell Gavette. Delcarpio and Gavette and a dozen other pirates stopped where the creek bed met the jungle. Spike and Moon watched as the two captains discussed a matter for a moment, before Delcarpio and three of his mates started up the creek. Gavette and his men returned to the shade of a large palm opposite the lagoon from where Spike and Moon were hiding in the bushes.

"This must be Delcarpio's Island," Moon whispered to Spike.

"Gavette must've fished the Carp out of the sea, and now he's going to collect his reward for being so kind and considerate," said Spike.

Moon and Spike retreated back into the jungle to shadow Delcarpio and his men up the dry sandstone creek bottom. The four Frenchmen wound around a few bends and then entered the jungle where an old weather-beaten and snarly trunked Caribbean pine hung out over the creek bed like an ancient battle-weary sentinel.

Following Delcarpio into the thick coppice, Moon and Spike eased their way in the direction of the French captain's angry voice. They found Delcarpio yelling at his men as they dug with their shovels. The French pirates dug a few feet to some wooden planks that covered a shallow pit. Delcarpio dropped down in the hole and lifted out a chest and two partially filled oilskin sacks.

Delcarpio continued his French tirade as he and his men covered the pit again and headed back to the creek and lagoon, toting the chest and oilskin sacks. Delcarpio didn't stop complaining until he was within hearing distance of Gavette.

When Gavette and his men noticed the returning French pirates, they hurried to meet them, eager to help them with their loads.

"Merci, bon ami," said Armand Delcarpio, forcing a smile as one of Gavette's men relieved him of an oilskin sack.

The French pirate captain took Russell Gavette aside, near where Moon and Spike were eavesdropping in the bushes.

"Monsieur Gavette, it is infortune that thees is all I have to . . . how yew say . . . 'reimburse.'"

"Repay. Well, it must suffice," Gavette said with a smirk.

"Oui, mon ami, infortune . . . my reserves are no more . . ."

"Yesss?" Gavette wanted the irritating Frenchman to get to the point.

"As you know, I was transporting ahhh . . . English aristocrat."

"Lady Sarah Howard."

"Mais puis zee good for no-thing Maxwell . . ."

"Took her, and now somebody else has her."

"Oui, oui. I was to take Lady Howard to a place. Peutêtre . . . maybe zee thief knows zat place, no?"

"And you were thinking maybe we should become partners, you and I: your knowledge and my ship. Not a bad idea. Where is this place you think they might be taking the Lady Howard?"

"We do business, then? One and one?"

"I'll be doing all the work. Two and one. Me two, you one," insisted Gavette.

Delcarpio failed to keep a look of disappointment from clouding his haggard face. "I must accept."

"So, where do we go from here?" Gavette asked.

"Trinidad. Take me to Trinidad, and then I show yew."

"Port of Spain," said Spike to Moon, when Gavette's longboat was on its way back to the *Rhinehart*. "It's got to be Port of Spain where Lady Howard is, or will be. We've got to tell the captain!"

"How?" said Moon. "He's way up in Nassau, too far for the longboat."

"We could head east for Long Island and Clarence Town, and take a ship from there."

"If a ship is going to Nassau from there, but what are them odds? And if there still *is* a Clarence Town."

Clarence Town was a small, recently established English settlement. There were many such ventures in the West Indies founded by well-meaning groups of Euro-

peans seeking political or religious freedom. But few efforts lasted long, most ended when the settlers realized
the hardships involved in creating an idealistic society out
of a stubborn wilderness. The discouraged settlers joined
already existing island townships elsewhere in the Caribbean, or they returned to Europe, or they perished.

"Do you suppose the Carp was telling the truth about
that being the last of his loot here on the island?" Moon
wondered aloud.

* * *

The two walked back around the island for the longboat.
They sailed it to the lagoon, and then journeyed up the
creek again to Delcarpio's pit, determined to find out if
any treasure remained.

"Well, well," said Spike, mimicking Delcarpio's French
accent, "cood it be that Me-sohr Carp is a lie-yahr?" They
had just removed one of the planks from the hole, reveal-
ing a treasure chest.

But they found only the one chest and two oilskin sacks.

"Buzzard guts!" Moon cursed after dumping one of the
oilskins out on the ground, making a pile of mostly Byz-
antine copper cookware, battered and tarnished green
with age. The objects would fetch a good price if presented to the right buyer; but a pirate appreciated only

the glitter of gold, silver, and precious stones.

Spike had better luck. The chest was overflowing with a wonderful assortment of goodies; Spike and Moon gazed raptly on a sapphire-studded gold chalice, a silver coronet with diamonds embedded in it, carved ivory images of African animals, topaz and olivine rings, pearl necklaces, a velvet pouch containing cut garnet and emeralds, and another pouch holding polished onyx and carnelian. Spike poured some of the gems out into his hand and slowly tilted the stones back and forth so that they sparkled in the sunlight like only precious stones can. And then there were the coins: sacks of gold, silver, copper, nickel and bronze moneys of various sizes and shapes and weights from several countries.

Moon dumped the contents of the other oilskin to find some more copper cookware.

"Devil dice!"

"We could use one of them pots to cook supper in tonight," Spike needled his large friend.

Moon growled. He picked up a pan and tried unsuccessfully to rub some of the green tarnish off on his shirtsleeve; then he rummaged through the other copper items, trying to find something of value.

There was a copper soap dish in the shape of a scallop shell that Moon couldn't open with his hands; taking a closer look he saw that—besides being tarnished green and having a few uninteresting ornamental etchings—the top and bottom of the shell were soldered shut. He held the dish up to his ear and shook it to see if it would rattle.

Nothing.

He took his dagger from his belt and tried to pry the shell-halves apart.

No luck.

Frustrated, Moon walked over to a hardwood tree and threw the soap dish at its trunk. The dish popped open and out flew a green-streaked white wad of cotton.

"Hey, look at that!" said Moon, proud of himself. He picked the ball of fluff up off the ground. "It's got something hard in it."

Moon unwound the cotton cloth to reveal a Pigeon-Blood ruby the size of a bar of soap!

Spike whistled, which was strange. Spike had tried his whole life to whistle and had never been able to; he could only manage, at best, the sound of wind blowing through a canyon. But now he was slicing the air as sharply as any parrot.

That night after supper, sitting by the campfire and looking up at the twinkling stars, Spike asked his best mate: "Suppose the Carp knew he had the stone?"

"I doubt it," said Moon. "He would've kept it close—not buried someplace."

"But where would you keep something like that?"

Neither Moon nor Spike had as yet referred to the notorious ruby by name, half-hoping it wasn't the Irrawaddy Stone after all, because of the reputation it had for causing its possessor bad luck. It was also famous for not staying put for very long; the Irrawaddy Stone had changed hands often, residing in most regions of the world.

Moon was holding the ruby close, afraid to let it out of his sight. "That would explain why it hasn't been seen for a while."

"How's that?" asked Spike.

"The Carp had it and didn't know it. It's been buried here for who knows how long?"

"What's that?" Spike teased, turning his head slightly as if to look into the realm of darkness outside the confines of the campfire.

"What?" Moon stood up, thinking Spike had heard something.

"No. I mean what were you talking about?"

"The stone!"

"What stone is that?"

"Here, catch!" Moon mimed throwing the giant ruby at Spike.

* * *

The next morning, Moon and Spike dug a new home for the treasure, keeping out a few gems, some money, and the Irrawaddy Stone. They cleaned up Delcarpio's pit to make it look like it hadn't been disturbed: a surprise for the returning Frenchman.

They decided to sail for New Providence and Nassau instead of Long Island and Clarence Town. It wasn't going to be an easy trip in the longboat, especially if the weather misbehaved, but the two agreed they would rather take a chance on the long run than on an uncertain, less direct route.

chapter 8

NASSAU

It was the hot, leaf-shriveling time of the afternoon on New Providence Island when Maxwell and his men finally reached Nassau from Delaport Point. It had been a long trek on foot over a hot and dusty road for the privateers. These were men not used to much walking.

Seven crewmen accompanied Maxwell: Wesley Tuttle, Zak Drago, Cory Heath, Emmett Sedgwick, Kipp Rafferty, Sheck Tilley, and Toby Gant. Not wanting to draw attention to themselves when they entered Nassau, they disbanded at the edge of town and rendezvoused in the alley behind the Lost Anchor. The Lost Anchor was a dockside tavern belonging to Simon "Codfish" Oglesby, an old acquaintance of Thatch Fitz-Henry and the *Hargus*, and then Jacob Maxwell and the *Bernadette*.

After finding the tavern free of spooks, Maxwell and his men made themselves at home, ravenously wolfing down several helpings of conch chowder, rye bread, and ale.

"My poor dogs are on the verge of mutiny," complained Cory, wiggling his fat toes. He was sitting on the floor with his back against the wall, boots off and legs sprawled. His feet had a right to rebel, having to carry so much more weight than the average pair.

Maxwell sat at a window seat in order to survey the harbor. Nassau didn't have a bay, but an offshore island a few hundred meters out gave ships shelter from heavy seas. "Any ships come in today, Codfish?" Maxwell's eyes rested on the *Catlow*, moored enticingly before him in the harbor.

"The *Belfast*. A couple of her mates came by here earlier. Inquired as to your health, Cap'n." The old salt laughed. Codfish could tell a tale, its tallness depended on the time of day and how freely his imagination happened to be running. Seldom one to volunteer information, Codfish was often unsure in memory and always careful to be dishonest to no one. "I told 'em about the last time you good-for-nothings was in here and started complaining about my pudding, and how I swabbed the deck with the lot of ya! I do hope that Moon recovered from the terrible beating I put him through. I didn't mean to be so rough on the little fella; I get kind of carried away at times."

"I think he'll live." Maxwell smiled and tried to mean it. "The *Catlow* came in yesterday?"

"That she did."

"How many smithies you got in this town?"

"Six to ten, maybe?"

Second in size to Havana in the Caribbean, Nassau was by far the most active of the port cities, forever reshaping herself. Although one of the oldest settlements in the islands, Nassau had an aura of impermanence about her. People were always coming and going or passing through. It was a boom town that kept on booming. But she seemed predestined to fold at any time and disappear; even the longtime residents of Nassau were always in a hurry, with a plan to move on soon. Nobody took a Sunday stroll in the park. There were no parks. There were several temporary buildings, a few old ones, some new. It would not surprise Maxwell—or any other salt familiar with the Bahamas—to someday approach Nassau and find her gone, discover that she had finally done what she always seemed to be threatening to do: pack up and leave.

The Spanish did their part in keeping Nassau on the verge of extinction. In retaliation for major losses in ships or cargo at the hands of a hostile country or pirates, the Spanish would often take their revenge on Nassau. The port city was conveniently situated near the Gulf Stream and not far from Havana, so the Spanish could send over a warship or two, or a few might swing out from an armada they were escorting and then lay havoc to the town. A Spanish warship would sometimes anchor and start blasting away just to try out a new cannon, or to test some ammunition.

The inconvenienced citizens of Nassau were accustomed to taking to the hills and waiting out the bombardments, and then, after the calamities, repairing whatever damage had been done.

"Ever hear the Carp mention any confederates of his here in Nassau?" Maxwell asked Zak Drago, sitting across the table from him.

"I heard he had several, but I know of none by name. When I signed articles with the *De la Cruz* in The Hague, I knew little of the ship or Monsieur Delcarpio. Most of the crew were new to the ship, except for the officers. I was looking for transport back to the Indies. Planned on leaving ship here, in Nassau, and making for the colonies up north. Never been there. Seen plenty of Nassau though, that's a fact."

"Know any blacksmiths?" asked Maxwell.

"Here in Nassau? A few, I reckon. Was a smithy in on the kidnapping?"

"Maybe." Maxwell preferred to have as few people as possible know about the Widow Archer's riddle, it might still prove to be only a couple of coincidences.

Maxwell sent his men out in pairs to investigate as many blacksmiths as they could find. They later returned to the Lost Anchor reporting no sign of Lady Howard nor of anyone from the *Catlow.*

Toby Gant and Wesley Tuttle followed a couple of *Belfast* crewmen around awhile, but this had led to nothing but a few pubs.

At one point in the search, Maxwell thought he and Emmett had come across something when the doctor-cook suddenly froze in his tracks and pointed at a sign swinging in the breeze in front of the Isabella Public House.

"A queen ain't a queen when she's a lodge!" Emmett had exclaimed.

"How's that?"

"Isabella was the queen who sent Columbus on his way; all us men of fortune owe a great debt to that grand lady."

"And you think maybe Lady Howard is being held in there somewhere?" The Isabella hadn't looked to Maxwell like the kind of place a kidnapper would be holding a captive, being right in the middle of town, along a main thoroughfare, and wearing a new coat of whitewash. If Maxwell were going to hide someone, he would choose someplace more out of the way, secluded.

"I thought the queen was a ship," said the captain, later

at the Lost Anchor, when Emmett suggested that since Lady Howard hadn't been found at any of the smithies, they should go back and search the Isabella.

"Well," said the doctor-cook, "who's to say she can't be a lodge—or anything else for that matter?"

"Or nothin' at all!" blared the captain, less concerned now if anybody heard him. "That blacksmith clue didn't do us much good, now did it! The business with Haylock and his black heart could've been a fluke; we probably would've spotted the *Mary Ann* anyhow!"

"I'll reconnoiter the place, Cap'n," said Zak. "I know a gentleman who used to lodge at the Isabella. I'll go see if he's still about, and look the place over."

"Wouldn't hurt, Cap'n," insisted Emmett.

"Go ahead," growled the captain, glaring out the window at the *Catlow* sitting tantalizingly on the water. How susceptible would the *Catlow* be to a night attack? Maxwell would dearly love to turn the tables on the scoundrels who had paid the *Bernadette* a visit! And darkness was fast approaching.

Dinner was soon to be served at the Isabella Public House, and a few folks were already sitting at tables when Zak approached a lady in the parlor who bore an air of authority. "Does a Wallace Winthrop still lodge here, ma'am?" he asked, removing his rag cap from his head.

"Will that be one more for dinner?"

"No, ma'am, I partook of my supper elsewheres."

"Room 3, then, and tell Mr. Winthrop that dinner is ready when he is."

"Thank you, ma'am, that I will."

Zak came upon Wallace Winthrop leaving his room. The more than middle-aged gentleman was working at locking his door, his hand shaking noticeably.

"Hard aport, Wally!" Zak called out as he came down the hall.

Wally Winthrop jumped to attention, but relaxed once he saw it was Zak who was shouting the order. "Why, Mr. Drago! You stayin' here at the Isabella?"

"Actually, I come to see you."

Wally was vaguely surprised; it had been a while since anybody had sought him out. He was a long time between jobs—not that he was actively in pursuit of employment. Wally would rather lean up against a bar and reminisce about old times and other places with a thirsty friend or stranger. And, although a companion was preferred for one of Wally's sojourns into alcoholic indulgence, he or she wasn't required.

"I was just on my way to supper," said the old salt. "Join me, then."

"I've already eaten, but I'll join ye in a pint."

"Two pints and a bowl of your famous potato soup, Mrs. Collins," said Wally, as he and Zak took a seat at one of the smaller and more private tables in the parlor.

Wally downed half his pint upon receiving it, and almost at once the trembling in his hands subsided. Wally had long passed the point in his life where a drink was a reward for his labors: it was now a necessity.

"Seems like the only thing I can stomach these days," he told Zak, referring to the creamy potato soup. "You still with the *Falcon?*"

"She went down in the Battle of Brest."

"I heard that was a good fight."

"I'm under the *Bernadette*'s sail now."

"Jacob Maxwell!" Wally was impressed. "You know, I sailed with Captain Thatch Fitz-Henry, but that was back before Maxwell come aboard."

"I recall you tellin' me a few tales."

"Cap'n Thatch gave me my name, back then, when I first started to really live! I was a young buck on an old Dutch merchantman, up near Nantucket, when we came under attack from the *Hargus*. I thought I was a goner for sure, and I would've been but for a lucky blow on my part, bringing down my adversary and namesake: Wallace Winthrop . . ."

"Wally?" Zak had to interrupt Wally's reminiscence. He knew that if he didn't stop the old salt, he would be in for Wally's entire life story, something Zak had already heard more than once and didn't have time to hear again.

Wally refocused his thoughts on the matter at hand. "But then where's the *Bernadette*, if you're here?"

"I'm doing some business for the captain."

"Oh?" Wally hoped there might be a little something in it for him; his reserves being a bit low. "How can I be of service?"

"Have you noticed the *Catlow* in the harbor?"

"Aye." Wally tried to remember if he'd heard anything about the ship or her crew. "I don't know what she's about, but I can find out soon enough."

"Have you heard any stories concerning white women?"

"There now, I heard there was a beauty being sold at auction tomorrow. Was thinking of attending myself. You know, I'm not getting any younger. Thought of maybe buyin' me a wife and takin' her up to the colonies, but with my swag bein' so depleted and all . . ."

Zak took a small blue sapphire from his belt and laid it on the table. "I've got to be running along; there's one more stone if you can find out anything about the *Catlow*. I'll come by again tomorrow, around noon."

"Sure thing, mate." Wally was obliged, the sapphire was good for several more months of easy living.

"It can't be Lady Howard," said Maxwell, shaking his head, after Zak reported to him at the Lost Anchor. "She'd be worth far more as ransom."

"But a lot less trouble," said Emmett. "Why not pass

THE PRIVATEER: A PIRATE FOR THE QUEEN

her off to somebody who's more willing to deal with the British crown?"

"But if the authorities see the woman is the Lady Howard, they'd arrest the ones trying to pass her off, wouldn't they?" argued Maxwell.

"Who's gonna know who she is? And what official has been born that can't be bought?" said Zak.

"What time is the auction tomorrow, Codfish?" Maxwell asked the bartender.

"Usually starts around 9 or so."

* * *

Maxwell and his crew slept on crates in the alley that night. Come sunrise they were already milling around the auction yard; Maxwell wanted to see who brought what slave to sell. Some slaves were already in the outside holding pen. Most of them were African. There were also a few Chinese, and one Arawak Indian.

Maxwell was familiar with the place, having had to bail out a few lads once who happened to fall into the wrong company. He knew the white woman would be locked up in one of the cells inside, where they held the more valuable or dangerous properties. There was also a small arena inside for when it rained, but usually the auctions took place out in the yard.

Slave buyers and sellers began arriving as the hour of 9 o'clock approached. It was a good showing, with many aristocrats in attendance. Ordinarily it was just the plantation foremen who came to buy and sell or exchange slaves.

As always there were a number of curious spectators and street vendors.

Maxwell bought himself and his men some sausages on sticks and started wandering around the throng of people gathering around the arena, looking for a good spot to watch the proceedings.

The auctioneers led out the slaves who were being held inside, one after the other, chained together by wrist manacles. The buzz of the crowd quieted a moment as everybody stopped to watch the parade, but then the buzz picked up again as folks started mumbling about how much they might be willing to bid on a particular property.

Maxwell dropped his sausage when he saw Sarah Howard at the end of the string of slaves being ushered into the holding pen. She sat down on a bench in the viewing cage, her head bowed, looking sad and humiliated.

"I don't believe it!" Maxwell muffled his astonishment with a hand over his mouth. He turned to Emmett and whispered, "Why does she not say who she is?"

Speechless, Emmett shook his head, trying to think. He finally offered: "Maybe she don't know where she is, maybe she's thinking nobody would give a diddle if they knew or not!"

"And me with barely a shekel!" Maxwell cursed, fumbling in his pockets, finding only a few pieces of silver and a couple of gemstones. "If the *Bernadette* were in port . . ." The captain suddenly realized what he had to do, and he whispered his plan to Emmett, "We'll just wait and see who buys Sarah and then relieve them of Her Ladyship on the way home."

Maxwell and his crew attempted to surreptitiously make eye contact with Sarah, but she was keeping her head downcast, staring dejectedly at the floor of the holding pen.

The auctioneers saved Lady Howard for last; most of the morning was gone before she was finally put up on the block.

"And now, ladies and gentlemen, what we have all been waiting for: a lovely creature of the finest breeding, intelligence, and grace. She can read and write. Sew and embroider. She can speak Spanish, English, and even a little French." The auctioneer pulled at Sarah's chains, encouraging the sullen young lady to turn around in a circle on the block. "Take a look at her assets, gentlemen! Spry. Well groomed.

"Shall we begin the bidding at ten gold pieces?"

Most of the slaves before Sarah had gone for between three and five gold pieces. A Chinese gentleman sold for seven, but that was because he came with papers certifying him as an expert jeweler. A good jeweler was rare in the New World outside of South America and Spanish control.

"Ten gold pieces!" said many voices at once.

"Twelve!" said one.

"Fifteen!" came quickly thereafter.

The bids climbed rapidly to thirty gold pieces before the wishful thinkers fell by the wayside and the serious money took charge.

"Thirty-five gold pieces!" said a rotund gentleman wearing a thick, official-looking English red overcoat that was much too heavy for a subtropical climate but too splendid to keep hanging in a closet. A huge black-and-white-striped three-pointed hat sat on top his oversized head and gave little shade to his delicate European complexion. The plump gentleman made frequent use of a handkerchief he was holding, dabbing the beads of sweat forming on his eminent brow.

"Forty gold pieces!" called out a coachman sitting high in the driver's seat of a stately carriage at the back of the crowd. Maxwell had noticed the carriage arrive earlier; it concealed an occupant who, for the first time, now offered a bid, relaying it through his coachman.

"Fifty!" came from a battered-looking rogue, exhibiting—on his leathery skin—facial scars from more fights won than lost, who was most likely carrying around even greater wounds under his tattered garments. No stranger to the sea, he audaciously spit a tobacco-tainted splat onto the sawdust-covered ground, letting everyone know he was unimpressed with the previous bids and with those who had made them.

"Tommy O'Neill!" Maxwell whispered to Emmett, recognizing the scalawag, a heartless man with too independent a mind to be trusted as a crew member.

"I thought he was dead!" Emmett whispered back.

"Fifty-five!" said the large round gentleman with a handkerchief at his cheek.

"Sixty-five!" The rogue spat again.

"Seventy-five!" called out the coachman.

"Eighty gold pieces!" said the redcoat, as he readjusted his three-pointed hat.

"One hundred!" The crowd murmured excitedly when the tobacco-chewing scalawag reached that figure. No plantation of slaves had ever gone for so much!

"One twenty!" The coachman had to shout to be heard above the excited crowd, which, upon hearing his bid, doubled its expression of amazement.

"This is my first, last, and only offer!" bellowed a mountain of a man, pushing aside the crowd. The huge new-comer showed off a wad of paper he held high in his hand as he walked up to the auctioneer.

It was Moon! He unfolded the map of Gavette's Island, and out spilled the Irrawaddy Stone with a thud on the auctioneer's table.

The crowd fell silent, spellbound, as a glistening red-dish hue emanated from the giant ruby, like genius recognized in a work of art, exciting imaginations.

The stone of incorporeal fire was indeed a queen's ransom!

The rogue cursed and stormed off.

The coachman put his reins to his horse, and the mysterious carriage retreated.

The overheated fat man fell to his knees. "Some water if you please!" he begged.

chapter 9

BACK TO THE BERNADETTE

W hat are you two doing in Nassau!" exclaimed Captain Maxwell, slapping Moon on the back in hearty appreciation. He had joined Moon and Spike at the auctioneer's table; Sarah was still standing on the auction block, looking around in a daze, as if she were unsure of where she was—hardly the look of a damsel just delivered from the wretched jaws of forced servitude.

The crowd was rapidly dispersing, becoming individuals again.

"We came to find you, Cap'n," said Spike, "to say that we knew where Lady Howard might be. You can imagine our surprise when we come up the street and see Her Ladyship standing on the block."

"Let's get down from there, then, Your Ladyship," said Maxwell. He and Moon helped her down. The captain became concerned with Sarah's continuing somberness, had she been drugged?

"I'm so confused, Captain," she mumbled, chin quivering, her eyes near tears. "I must speak with you."

There was nobody remaining in the yard other than Sarah and the *Bernadette* lads; the auctioneers had taken their chains, money, and ruby inside. "It's all over now, ma'am," the captain reassured her. "You go right ahead and say whatever ye please."

Sarah looked anxiously about the yard. "Not here," she insisted. "Someplace else, more private."

Maxwell and his men escorted Sarah quickly to the Lost Anchor.

Finally satisfied that only the right ears would be hearing what she had to say, Sarah humbly bowed her head again, and confessed, "I'm not the Lady Howard." She took in the look of shock on the buccaneer's faces, and then explained, "I'm Rebecca, Rebecca Webb. The person you knew as me is really Sarah Howard. When Armand Delcarpio attacked our ship, I insisted that Sarah and I exchange identities to protect her. This deception worked up until our abduction by Razmus Foote and his confederate; this man knew who Sarah was."

"That would be Sparano," Maxwell grumbled.

"I've seen him before," said Rebecca, "on more than one occasion. I can't remember where, for certain—someplace in London, I think."

She looked at Moon with sorrowful eyes. "I'm sorry you had to lose your lovely ruby on my account, but they promised harm to Sarah if I complained." Rebecca was about to cry again.

"That's all right, miss. It was beginning to burn a hole in my pocket anyhow."

Spike gave Moon a hard slap across the shoulder. "As if it was *your* stone to be giving away!"

"Like I said!" Moon growled at Spike. "It was burnin' a hole in me pocket!"

"Hey, Captain," Emmett just realized, "a queen is not a queen when . . ."

"Stow it, Emmett!" Maxwell had had his fill of riddles and of things being other than what they should.

"But why was it necessary for me to stay quiet? Or even live?" Rebecca wondered. "Why didn't they just let me go or kill me? They had Sarah."

"That was for my benefit," said Maxwell, going to the window for yet another look at the *Catlow*. A ship with familiar sails, the *Horn*, was coming in from the sea. Maxwell had planned to use the *Bernadette*'s longboat—compliments of Moon and Spike—to return to Delaport Point, but he realized any attempt to exit the harbor now would be challenged. "Any ships leave port this morning?" he asked Codfish.

"The last ship I seen depart was the *Hathaway*, and that was yesterday, before you got here."

Maxwell turned back to Rebecca. "Vernon Tate, the captain of the *Catlow*, is an ornery old salt, but he would have no part in doing you or any other woman harm. And I'm just as certain the *Catlow* is sitting out there without the company of Lady Howard or Razmus Foote. I'd wager Vernon Tate is out there twiddling his thumbs, wondering what became of Mr. Foote, who no doubt told Tate yesterday that he would be back shortly for a sail off to someplace else.

"The *Catlow* is being used—the same as you, Rebecca, to throw me and everybody else off the trail. I'd put my money on the devil and Sarah Howard being halfway to England with the *Hathaway*."

"Maybe not," said Moon, and he told the captain about the deal he and Spike had heard Delcarpio make with Russell Gavette.

"Foote also mentioned Trinidad," said Rebecca, "but I'm not sure what it was in reference to. Something to do with money. All they ever talked about was money."

Should Maxwell head out across the Atlantic or go south to Trinidad in pursuit of the *Hathaway*? He should call a halt to the whole affair! Cut his losses and return to simple buccaneering. But how could he do that now? Every fire rat on the sea believed Maxwell held Lady Howard again. Maxwell decided to wait until he got himself, his men, and Rebecca back to the *Bernadette* before thinking about what to do next. For now, he must concern himself with getting back.

"Looks like we got company, Cap'n," said Toby Gant at the window. At least a dozen pirates were making their way up the harbor front.

"Let's make for the western highway, lads!" ordered the captain.

Before exiting into the back alley, Maxwell hung one of Codfish's bar towels from the end of his saber and stuck it out the door as he swung it open. The roar of exploding muskets filled the air, and at least one musket ball found its mark as the cloth flew off Maxwell's sword.

Maxwell and his men rushed from the tavern before their adversaries had time to reload their firearms.

Kipp Rafferty discharged his pistol—one of two the *Bernadette* lads had with them—into a gang of sword-brandishing pirates running up the alley at them through a cloud of powder smoke. Musket pistols were accurate up to about as far as a man could spit, so Kipp didn't wait to see if he hit anything before drawing his sword and joining his mates in the dash to meet their attackers.

As he ran, Toby Gant aimed his pistol at the heart of one of the oncoming *Belfast* crewmen that he and Wesley Tuttle had followed around the day before. The shot blew off a good chunk of the man's ear, which flew into the face of the pirate running beside him.

Maxwell was the first to reach the pirates. And the clanging of steel striking steel, and the curses and cries of those wounded and enraged filled the alley.

Emmett had remained on the back porch of the Lost Anchor with Rebecca. He watched the beginning of the battle, and when he was certain his mates would make short work of their opponents, he took Rebecca's hand and led her down the alley, away from the fighting.

"Come on," said the doctor-cook to Rebecca, who, at first, was reluctant to follow. "The lads will be along shortly."

Indeed! The *Bernadette* privateers made known their unsurpassed swordsmanship, slashing their opponents' garments to tatters and their skin to the bone; their enemy soon took off running for the support of the main advance coming up the beach.

Maxwell and his crew hurried up a side street after Emmett and Rebecca, and then they ran down another alley—their pursuers not far behind.

"Hold up!" Maxwell shouted, halfway out of town. "Kipp, Spike, and Zak stays with me. The rest of you keep on going. Make for the highway. We'll give these scalawags a chase and catch up with you later."

When Rebecca and the others were out of sight, Maxwell, Kipp, Spike, and Zak stepped back into the street and ran for the next corner. The horde of trailing marauders entered the street just in time to see the backsides of the four *Bernadette* privateers making the turn.

"They went thataway!" Maxwell shouted at one point when the mob of pirates had slowed down, unsure of where to go. Maxwell and his men kept their pursuers interested with glimpses of themselves darting in and out of doorways and alleys, with the sound of their boots running up and down boardwalks, with taunts from windows and rooftops.

Shortly after dusk, and after several near captures by the frustrated pirates, the trail of the privateers again went cold at the empty marketplace in the center of town. Here a maze of shacks and stalls and stables made any further search seem futile. The pirates spread out in one last effort to find Maxwell and Lady Howard before giving up.

Exhausted, Maxwell and his three fellow runarounds ran into Rebecca and the others only a short distance from Nassau; they were waiting by the side of the road, sitting on horses.

Maxwell flung himself against a tree, breathing heavily, and looked cockeyed at the strange sight of sailors on horseback.

"Where'd ye get them things?" he managed to say between pants.

"Why, Captain Maxwell!" joked Cory Heath, "We bought them, of course! You don't take us for a bunch of thieves, now do you?"

"This was Rebecca's idea, Cap'n," accused Emmett, sitting uncomfortably in the saddle, holding his reins awkwardly, one in each hand. This was the first time he had been on a horse, which was also true of the others.

"There's no problem," Rebecca reassured the unhappy men. "As I was saying, your horse will follow the ones with us who know how to ride."

"I hate horses!" Maxwell grumbled, climbing into one of four empty saddles. The captain had—on one other occasion—been on the back of a horse.

"Just give them a little kick," said Rebecca, as she expertly pranced her mount in a circle around the anxious men, before taking off in a lope down the road.

Zak, a good horseman, took up the rear. He let out a whistle or a whoop whenever one of the horses between Rebecca and himself would start to slow down.

It was a much faster trip going back to Delaport Point than it had been coming from there the day before. It was an unpleasant and noisy journey, however, with the buccaneers complaining all the while about how their backsides were suffering.

The nearly full moon lit up the *Bernadette* sitting majestically on the calm waters off Delaport Point. She was a welcome sight to her returning crewmen and their guest.

Brice Depwig and Link Spivey had come ashore to meet their captain and fellow mates, and they greeted Rebecca with an enthusiasm that was undiminished when they learned that she was, in fact, Miss Webb and not Lady Howard.

"Everything go all right at Rum Cay?" Maxwell asked, after he had carefully slid down off his mount.

"Aye, sir," said Depwig, the *Bernadette*'s helmsman. "No trouble. We dropped anchor here about an hour ago."

The buccaneers relieved the horses of their gear and gladly set them free. And after taking more comfortable seats in the bumboats, the crewmen rowed with sanguine strokes out to their beloved ship.

chapter 10

DOWN THE BANK

Few people are more superstitious than a sailor, particularly a pirate. And this could best be observed on deck the vessels sailing the Great Bahama Bank during the time of the buccaneers. The Great Bahama Bank is the submerged carbonate platform on which the hard coral heads of the Bahama Islands rest. The depth of the sea over the Kansas-sized bank is seldom greater than thirty meters and usually less than twenty—bearing untold hundreds of spots where a bit of sand, rock, or coral lies within easy reach of the hull of an unwary ship.

The *Bernadette* was a wary ship. She had made the run up and down the treacherous bank numerous times without so much as a scrape on her keel. These runs generally took place during the day, of course: a captain would have to be either a fool or in dire straits to expose his vessel to the hazard of sailing the Bahama waters at night.

And there were few mindless pirate captains, but most of them at one time or another found themselves praying for the cover of darkness whilst being hounded by a Spanish warship or two.

Fortunately, the *Bernadette* had Ivy Sabin as her lookout, no other ship's lookout was so keen of sight or so clever. Ivy kept an ever-expanding map and mental history of every shoal and rock pinnacle the *Bernadette* encountered on her journeys. He possessed a remarkable sense of time and position that carried over into the darkest of nights and the foulest of weather.

If the *Bernadette* had to be under way at night, the captain gave Ivy a man or two at the bow to help keep watch. But there were always more men atop the forecastle than those required by the captain; the lads liked to linger by the bow cannon; it was a favorite place to have a smoke or chew and tell tales while keeping an eye on where their ship was heading.

"One point to starb'rd, Mr. Depwig," Ivy called down to the helmsman.

The lads at the bow—and everybody else on deck—looked to port to see the snag the *Bernadette* was trying to avoid.

"There," said Toby Gant, pointing to a piece of sea some fifty meters out that was murkier than the rest: a reef or a sand bank looming just below the surface. The motion of the ship on the rolling swells gave life to the approaching giant shadow; a seemingly evil presence, like a monster in the moonlight poised to spring from its hiding place beneath the waves. The lads crossed themselves and spit, and mumbled an oath or a prayer.

"Two points to port." Ivy readjusted the ship's heading after the danger had passed.

Emmett Sedgwick was down in the galley, sitting at the table, mulling over the Widow Archer's riddle as Egan Shaw and Billy Fry went about cleaning up after the evening mess. The ship's doctor-cook didn't like the way his captain had spoken disparagingly of the riddle back in Nassau. It was obvious to Emmett that some manifestations of the portent had already come to pass.

"It's that part about the blacksmith that's got me stumped," said Emmett.

"The widow must've been referring to Trinidad, not Nassau," replied Egan, who was at the washtub with Billy; both of the young men were elbow deep in soapsuds.

Emmett, deep in thought, drew heavily on his pipe.

"Tell us about the ruby again, Emmett," said Billy.

"The Irrawaddy Stone? As big as a fist it was. Impressive? Took everybody's breath away! But we are best rid of the cursed thing."

"I can't understand that," said Billy.

"It's the history of the thing, bringing bad luck wherever it goes. Moon did right in passing it off to somebody else."

"Where did it come from?" Egan asked.

"The highlands of Burma, a long, long time ago. Legend has it a Burmese prince destroyed a whole village to get his hands on the giant ruby, and then had it mounted as the crowning jewel in a grand headpiece on a marvelous throne of gold and gems. The prince soon came to a bad end and his throne was dismantled and lotted out. The fabulous ruby was passed around them maharajas down in India for a while, where it got its reputation for bringing bad luck. They say the Irrawaddy Stone won't rest till it's back in the village whence it came."

Billy said, "So then why would anybody want it? I mean, if it brings nothin' but bad luck?"

"Because men are fools! Thinking they can outwit or befriend the powers that possess the stone."

"What if you got a hold of the ruby and promised to take it back to the village it came from, would it bring you good luck, then, instead of bad?" Egan wondered.

"Make a deal with a bloody rock?" Billy laughed. "That's the stupidest thing I ever heard!"

Up on the poop deck, Captain Maxwell pointed out a shooting star to Rebecca. They were leaning against the rail and talking about the ship's journey, when they were distracted by what sounded like somebody dropping a stack of dishes down below in the galley. Another similar crashing sound followed immediately thereafter. And then all was quiet again.

Maxwell shrugged his shoulders and continued explaining to Rebecca: "The *Hathaway* started out a day and a half and one night ahead of us. If she played it safe— believing no one was aft her—she would've found anchorage last night and again tonight, so by morning we should be within half a day's reach. And that's if she come down the bank, like us. She most likely headed up through the Northeast Channel and is now on her way down the Atlantic side—bypassing the islands altogether, which would have been the smart thing to do, and what I hope she's done. There's no need to anchor out there on the Atlantic, but we can be a day ahead of her to Trinidad."

It was difficult for Maxwell to regard Rebecca as herself and not Lady Howard. She had played the role of a royal convincingly. Did Rebecca have royal blood? Jacob wondered. It was common for the further removed members of the royal family to possess a title but little financial means. The male members of these less privileged royals usually took military or clerical positions for their subsistence; the female ones married into money and were often companions to richer cousins in their youth.

"Are you related to Lady Howard?" Maxwell asked.

Rebecca replied, "No, My mother was a seamstress for Sarah's mother, who was very kind to us. Sarah and I are nearly the same age, and we were brought up together. I grew up believing Sarah was my little sister and, really, I still do."

"It must have been an eye opener the day you learned your sister was worth more than yourself—heir to so much more privilege."

"From whose point of view? My mother's? Sarah's mother's? Mine? Do you not value the lives of your family more than your own?"

"I never had a family."

"I'm sorry."

"There's nothing to be sorry about; it's not like I lost one."

"A friend, then?"

Jacob Maxwell thought of Russell Gavette and the companionship they had shared while growing up, how the harsh existence was easier to survive with Russell to count on. And Jacob recalled the sorrow and loss he had suffered with his friend's betrayal.

"That's different," he growled. "A mate will always stand up for a fellow mate or he ain't worth his salt! And won't be long on the *Bernadette!*"

Spike came up behind Moon, who was swapping tales with some of the other lads at the bow cannon. They were all helping keep watch, looking ahead into the depths of the night waters.

Two guns made up the bow cannon, one on each side of the bowsprit. The men regarded the guns less as battle artillery than as objects to lean against or sit upon. The *Bernadette* was one of the few vessels not originally a warship to have a bow cannon, and another astern—these being an addition of firepower at the expense of canvas and speed.

"Moon," said Spike, "you know, when it comes down to it, Rebecca Webb belongs to Egan and Emmett, and you and me. It was our ruby that bought her from the slavers."

Moon laughed. "I'm sure the cap'n has something to say in the otherwise."

"It's the quartermaster you need to be speakin' to," said Link Spivey. "It's he decides matters concernin' shares, and that's what this is about."

"You're right, mate," said Spike, looking around. "So, have you seen our Harley around anywhere? There he is."

Harley Fenton was astern, by the starboard ladder on the quarterdeck, talking to Kipp Rafferty. Spike and Moon grabbed Harley and took him up to see the captain, who was still on the poop talking to Rebecca.

They asked the captain for his opinion.

"Sounds like a matter for the quartermaster, all right," agreed Maxwell.

"What would the Irrawaddy Stone be worth in gold?" Harley scratched his chin, beginning to calculate a figure.

"At least a queen's ransom," said Maxwell, giving Rebecca a wink. "No less than three hundred, I would guess."

"I was thinking more like five," said Moon.

Spike nodded his agreement.

The captain whistled.

"How about four, then?" said Harley. "That would be an even one hundred apiece."

"Sounds fair enough, I suppose," said Moon, and Spike agreed.

"And that would be coming out of the ship's shares?" asked Maxwell.

Quartermaster Fenton pondered the question a moment. "I think it should come from your shares, Cap'n. This being your business from the beginning. You can square it later with the royal court."

Maxwell groaned but didn't argue.

"Will we be stopping at Delcarpio's Island to pick up the rest of the treasure, Cap'n?" Spike asked. "It's right along the way."

"No, we can't spare a minute. We should stop at Port Royal to replace the longboat, too, but we can't afford the time to do that either."

* * *

After three nights' and two days' sail, the *Bernadette* had left the Great Bahama Bank behind, and was heading south through Mona Passage between the islands of Hispaniola and Puerto Rico. As they approached Mona Island in the middle of the channel, Ivy was surprised to see a Spanish warship anchored in the shallows.

"No sign of her crew, Cap'n," shouted Ivy, peering through his lens as the *Bernadette* closed in on the island and the other vessel. The warship's sails were struck. "She appears to be deserted."

"It's probably a trap," Maxwell grumbled to himself.

He shouted up to Ivy, "No sign of another warship?" Spanish war galleons seldom sailed alone, usually traveling in pairs if not escorting an armada of treasure galleons with a half-dozen sister warships.

"Looks like a trap!" Ivy warned. "She's sitting behind a reef that's going to chew up any hull that draws near!"

Maxwell ordered some men aloof to make it look as if the *Bernadette* were going to strike sail—which she did, when she was almost on top of the reef.

"Hard astarb'rd!" Maxwell commanded.

After a sharp turn without her sails, the *Bernadette*'s portside cannon sent a volley of fireballs at the Spanish vessel. Smoke and wood splinters exploded into the air. A host of sailors in blue-and-white Spanish naval uniforms appeared on deck the warship, running from the flames and jumping over her side into the water.

"Reload!" Maxwell was in a hurry because, just as he expected, the *Bernadette* was now heading straight for another warship that had come out from behind Mona Island. "Keep her headed straight for her bow, Mr. Depwig." And he shouted forward, "On my mark, bow cannon, into 'er sails!"

The two ships approached each other: the warship coming on fast with the wind at her back, the *Bernadette* coasting along without a sail.

"Fire!" Maxwell barked. The *Bernadette*'s bow cannon shot two perfectly round holes through the sails—one hole on each side of the three masts of the approaching warship.

The warship then fired her bow cannon, but the shots sailed harmlessly through the empty spaces between the spars of the *Bernadette*.

"Now set them sails!" Maxwell shouted aloft to the men on the spars, who started pulling out canvas as if their lives depended on it.

"Hard about, Mr. Depwig."

And as the *Bernadette* was making her turn, "Ready starb'rd cannon! Remember now, we only want 'er sails!" Maxwell waited for the right moment, for when the tilt of the beam would be at the required angle.

"Fire!"

A volley of mostly chain and grapeshot tore the on-coming vessel's sails to shreds, slowing the war galleon to a sudden crawl. Her foremast was severed—the top half blowing back into her mainmast rigging.

The *Bernadette* finished coming around, and with the recoil of her cannon adding to the wind now at her back, her bow plowed the waves for the first Spanish warship. On the privateer's pass, she emptied her starboard cannon into a crippled warship already on fire and soon to be sinking into the shallows.

Her sister warship, nearly dead in the water, with rags for sails, made a slow turn to port and aimed her starboard cannon at the *Bernadette* fast pulling away. The guns were lit, but in vain; the cast-iron cannon balls fell short, splashing harmlessly into the sea.

"Who do you suppose them gentleman were?" remarked Kipp to Sheck Tilley, as they cheered triumphantly along with the rest of the victorious *Bernadette* crew.

"Probably a bunch of raw recruits out of Havana, getting a lesson in seamanship," returned Sheck.

"Well, mate, I reckon we showed 'em a thing or two!"

chapter 11

THE MOUTH OF THE DRAGON

Columbus discovered the island of Trinidad during his last sally out from his command base on the island of Hispaniola in 1505, as he searched once again for the mainland of China. He named Trinidad for three large peaks he saw in a mountain range on the island's northern end; he called the mountains the Northern Range (at this point, Christopher Columbus was, understandably, running out of names to call things). As he sailed north of Trinidad, heading west for the South American continent (which he mistook in the distance as a small, flat, insignificant little island and so left it unnamed just as he had done earlier in the day with Tobago, on the other side of Trinidad), a mighty fog began rolling toward him from the south and over the bay separating Trinidad from the continent; the thick gray cloud rapidly engulfed a string of rock pinnacles jutting up out of the sea. And as the admiral witnessed this marvelous spectacle of nature, he imagined smoke bellowing out of the mouth of a giant dragon (the rock pinnacles being the dragon's teeth, of course).

Indeed! When the thick, rolling mist overtook his vessel and he could smell the unmistakable odor of sulfur in the water vapor, Columbus at once proclaimed the demonic strait the Mouth of the Dragon. He turned his ship around and hurried back to the safety of his base on Hispaniola, never to know, unto his death, that he had discovered a continent—not the one he had been looking for, but a hefty chunk of real estate, nonetheless.

Some years later, when gold and silver began flowing into the Spanish homeland from the New World, the king of Spain decided that Trinidad would make a good place for a fort and settlement to act as a stopover for treasure ships coming up the east coast of South America.

Legend has it King Carlos gave Ramon Gomez the governorship of Trinidad because His Majesty held a grudge against the Gomez family, and he was sending Ramon to the island as punishment. Actually, Ramon just happened to be in the room when the king came up with the idea. Neither King Carlos nor Ramon could know the hell awaiting the first governor of Trinidad.

Approaching their new home from the north, the Spanish settlers sailed down into the Mouth of the Dragon, and they were immediately surrounded by the same sort of low cloud that Columbus had discovered earlier. The settlers headed straight for shore and began building Port of Spain at the foot of the misty mountains by the foggy bay. A couple of months later, the haze lifted for the first time (for a few minutes), and the settlers got to see where they were.

Trinidad turned out to be mostly flat, an extension of the saltwater swamps dominating the east coast of Venezuela. There were the mountains in the Northern Range, and a few small hills rose in the south. A number of breathtaking waterfalls fell from the Northern Range to eventually feed a multitude of swamps in the flatland. Natural gas and petroleum bubbled up from the bowels of the Earth along with hot water to form steaming bogs. Separating the swamps from one another were mud volcanoes, tar and sulfur pits, and quicksand-corrupted stretches of thin ground.

The castle builders had to stop hauling stone down from the Northern Range when they ran out of slaves; or, rather, after the slaves ran away or were swallowed up by the swamps, along with most of the slave drivers. The favorite sport of the few Arawak Indians living on the island was to coax a male settler or slave into the bogs, using the alluring charms of an Indian princess dancing naked in the mist.

More African slaves were brought in to replace those who had vanished, but the ranks of these, too, were soon depleted. A shipload of Chinese were tried, but they disappeared faster than the Africans. Some natives of East India were abducted and delivered, but most of these died of the pox on the way.

By this time it had become obvious that the east side of South America had little gold or silver to offer, nothing compared with the rich deposits in Peru, Columbia, and Mexico. And so King Carlos decided Port of Spain wouldn't be needed as a stopover after all.

The castle was left unfinished.

All those who could, left the island, leaving only the Gomez family to prevail for Spain, and a handful of servants to support the Gomez family, and those who were not welcome anyplace else, and those lacking in ambition or bias.

And the monks.

Trinidad had been attracting Catholic monks from every corner of Europe, especially France; here they found the solitude and isolation they most cherished. Several monasteries were built hither and yon about the fog-shrouded swamps, and it came to pass that there were more monks on the island than anybody else. However, they were seldom seen. The monks kept to themselves and their monasteries, and they journeyed to Port of Spain only when it became necessary to trade for the few items essential in maintaining their austere existence.

Horses did not fare well on Trinidad, finding the swamps hard to avoid, especially at night. The monks brought a few donkeys with them to the island, and these beasts of burden proved better able to watch where they were going. Asses turned out to do an even better job than donkeys. Asses seemed to have a sixth sense of knowing when things weren't right in the way ahead, such as when a patch of quicksand had developed in a road traversing soft sand.

There are two species of ass in the world: the African, or true ass; and the Asiatic, or half-ass. Both species found their way to the island of Trinidad as beasts of burden. The half-ass came to a quicker stop than the true ass, and so was considered more intelligent. The true ass carried a heavier load, and so was considered more valuable, especially to the tobacco farmers on Trinidad—tobacco being the only cash crop able to grow on the island; that is, on the few acres that weren't under water, mud, or tar. The monasteries grew tobacco to trade as a supplement to their meager allotments from the church.

Unfortunately for the rider of an ass—no matter how fast an ass was traveling—upon encountering a hazard, the animal would come to an immediate halt. Naturally, the occupant of the saddle would go flying head over heels into whatever peril was awaiting: quicksand, mud, hot water, or tar.

The bruised, broken, and embarrassed victims of these tragedies would arrive in town or at a monastery covered head to toe in mud, sand, or tar; and, of course, the most frequent explanation given when asked what had happened, was, "It was the ass's fault!"

The ingredients of the tar pits (the most dreaded of all the hazards featured on this ill-starred island) came to be known as "the ass's fault," which was later shortened to "ass fault." Soon after arriving, a visitor to Trinidad would be advised to "Watch out for the ass fault" or "Be careful not to step in the ass fault."

In a letter of correspondence to his native land, an Irish Catholic monk mentioned the remarkable black gooey substance but spelled it with a Latin flavoring, and it became "asphalt."

Today, Trinidad remains a major supplier of asphalt to the world, and the island shows no indication of ever running out of the valuable commodity.

* * *

It was a foggy evening when the *Bernadette* arrived at the Mouth of the Dragon. She dropped anchor in a cavity of tooth number three—also known as the little rock island of Chacachacare.

Maxwell took seven of his men and two bumboats ashore. Egan Shaw and Billy Fry pleaded with their captain to let them go, too, but he said no—on four frustrating occasions—before the captain and the chosen ones rowed out of the tiny cove for the main island.

Egan whispered to Billy, who was standing next to him likewise watching the two bumboats fade into the mist and darkness, "There's still one more bumboat left!"

The two young men threw the last bumboat overboard and quickly climbed down the topside rope lattice before they could be stopped.

"What do you rascals think you're doing!" Emmett called out angrily from the rail.

"Just thought we'd do a bit of night fishin' before we turned in, Gov," Egan teased, as he and Billy paddled away.

"Turn about and get back here!" Emmett was concerned as well as angry.

"We'll bring ye back a big one!" Billy shouted to Emmett, who quickly disappeared from the lads' view in the foggy night.

It was pitch black! A shiver of fear shook Billy on the way to tooth number two. "This fog stinks!" he complained. How were they ever going to find their way ashore!

"Shhh!" insisted Egan. "Listen for the sound of the sea hitting up against the rocks, and make for it."

The surface of the Mouth of the Dragon was calm, the night quiet. The faint but unmistakable sound of water lapping rock reached the two lads in the dark. The lapping grew louder as they drew nearer and then almost collide with tooth number two; a wall of stark black stone rose from the bay, higher than the two lads could see, which wasn't very far.

Egan and Billy rowed around the large rock pinnacle and headed for tooth number one; and after that, the shore of the main island. They dragged their bumboat up the beach and came upon the ones Maxwell and the others had left. And then they followed a trail to a sandy road leading to Port of Spain.

"Look out for asphalt," Egan warned Billy as they walked along. Egan had been to Trinidad twice before. "And quicksand."

"What?"

Egan explained the many pitfalls awaiting the unwary traveler in Trinidad. "And we're going to have to avoid the cap'n, too!"

Billy agreed and added, "He's going to be trying to avoid being discovered hisself."

"Everybody is going to be looking out for everybody else," Egan concurred.

"In this stinking fog!" complained Billy, as they approached a smelly sulfur pit. Nearby was a mud volcano, its bursting bubbles sounded like large bullfrogs talking to one another.

After a while the mist began to glow a short distance ahead.

"Port of Spain," said Egan, pulling Billy to a halt. "So, what's the plan? We can't just go waltzing into town."

"Why not? Nobody knows us," said Billy.

"There's bound to be somebody we know, what with Gavette and the Carp and everybody else about! And we'd be blowin' Cap'n Maxwell's cover as well as our own!"

"In this fog? If by chance someone does make us, we'll just say we're by ourselves—from the other side of the island."

Egan was uneasy about it, but into town they strode, trying to look as if they knew where they were going.

The little shantytown did its best to reveal itself by burning Trinidad's abundant crude oil in elevated iron pots along its sandy streets. But the pots seemed to Billy and Egan to emit more smoke than light, just adding more weight to the lingering mist. There shone but a faint glow in the soot-smudged windows of the houses and huts they passed by.

The lads stopped to try to figure out what direction the sound of a honky-tonk piano was coming from. Egan noticed a livery stable across the street and it reminded him of the Widow Archer's riddle. He elbowed Billy.

"Hey, look! A blacksmith!"

They circled the stable and approached a small back window through an empty corral. Egan took a peek inside. Some lamps were burning.

"Don't look like anybody's in there," he whispered.

They went back around front and knocked. When no one came to the door, Billy tried the latch and the door opened. They called out as they ventured inside, "Hello? Blacksmith?"

They checked a storeroom and then the stalls.

"That is the ugliest horse I've ever seen!" exclaimed Billy, coming to a stop at one of the stalls.

"Those ain't horses! That's an ass," said Egan.

"So *that's* an ass."

"You ain't never seen an ass before?"

"I come from Virginia. We don't allow such ugly creatures on the road, fool."

"Don't *fool* me! If you was so smart, you'd know an ass when ya saw one." Egan pointed at a different ass in another stall. "See here? This is what they call a half-ass, you can tell it by the black mane and the line running down its back. They say these are smarter than those." Egan referred to the one Billy was standing in front of. "Those they call true asses."

"This is a dumb one? They both look dumb to me—almost as dumb as you!" Billy didn't like the way Egan was trying to one-up him with his knowledge of asses.

Egan stuck his proud and handsome face into Billy's. "And not near as ugly as you!"

Billy took a swing at Egan's head.

Egan ducked and gave Billy a push across the straw-covered floor. Billy hit up against the blacksmith's forge, which had a branding iron sticking in its hot bed of coals. Billy grabbed the iron and headed back toward Egan, waving the glowing red end of the rod as he came on the attack. He swung at Egan, who ducked again. The iron slammed into a post, rattling one of the oil lamps, nearly knocking it off its nail.

Egan grabbed a share of the iron, and the two wrestled each other to the floor, where they rolled over and over down the alley between the stalls.

Billy managed to stabilize himself on top of Egan, and he began to press the hot point of the iron closer and closer to Egan's cheek. Billy was going to give Egan a scar to forever remember him by, every time Egan would look in the mirror ...

But then came the sound of footsteps and muffled voices at the back door!

The two lads scrambled on their hands and knees across the floor toward the stalls, finding an empty one just as the large back door to the corral slid open.

To Billy and Egan's amazement, in walked the Lady Howard—known earlier to them as Rebecca Webb—her mouth gagged and her hands tied. She was accompanied by Razmus Foote, Frederick Sparano, and one other man.

The men took three asses out of the forward stalls and began saddling them.

"These beasts will take you directly to St. Joseph's," Foote said to Sparano. "The blacksmith told me they are used often by the monks of the monastery, and know the road by rote. You also have Mr. Campbell, here, who assures me he knows the way.

"It's been a while, but I reckon the monastery is still in the same place it was," Campbell chuckled, "but who knows in those swamps!" Jason Campbell was a crewman on the *Hathaway*; Razmus Foote recruited him after Foote learned that Campbell had lived a few years in Port of Spain.

"Do you know any of the monks at St. Joseph's?" Sparano asked Campbell.

"Not me! Nobody knows the monks. Give me the willies, they do. They could've chose a more pleasant spot to go lookin' for the Almighty—if you know what I mean!"

"Just ask for sanctuary for the night," said Foote. "I'll be along in the morning."

They led the asses out to the corral and slid the large door closed.

Billy and Egan started to get up but fell back down when Foote and Sparano came back inside. The men walked toward the two lads, Foote speaking in a low voice to Sparano, "There's been a change of plan; it seems Mr. Dudley no longer desires a ransom for his lady, but her death instead."

The two men stopped in front of the stall where Billy and Egan were hiding in a little bit of straw and even less shadow. For a brief, charged moment, neither man spoke. If either of them had looked intently into the stall, they probably would have seen the lads—but the criminals had other things on their minds.

Sparano said, "This will cost you more than the original twenty gold pieces we agreed upon."

"An extra ten, and you must also quiet our friend Mr. Campbell." Foote slid a finger across his throat, signifying that Jason Campbell must also die. "I am told there is a junction in the road not far from St. Joseph's Monastery, where a signpost points one way to St. Joseph's and the other to the Monastery of St. Pierre. Alongside the road is a swamp of unusual depth. It would be easy for a maiden and her abductor to fall victim to its treachery, especially at night."

"I understand," said Sparano.

"It is important that no marks suggesting foul play be found on Her Ladyship or her captor," added Foote.

"Of course," said Sparano.

The two men went into the storeroom and returned with hand torches. They used one of the oil lamps to light them before going back outside to the corral.

This time, Billy and Egan waited a minute before getting to their feet.

Then Billy rushed to the nearest stall that had an ass. "Hurry! We've got to go after them!"

Egan agreed, but he made no move to saddle an animal.

"What are you waiting for?" Billy barked.

"I don't know how to ride," Egan admitted with shame.

"What was all that talk about asses before?"

"I seen asses—I ain't never rode on one!"

"I just hope it's the same as riding a horse," said Billy.

Billy finished saddling his ass and then fixed one for Egan. They followed fresh hoof prints in the corral down a side street and out of Port of Spain.

Billy kicked his ass into an uncomfortably fast trot. Egan's animal followed.

The lights of Port of Spain quickly faded behind them. Billy couldn't see the road beneath his mount's pounding hooves; he crossed himself and uttered a prayer that the ass knew where it was going. A faint sliver of a moon could be seen now and then glowing faintly in the stagnant mist. There were no stars.

"Ouch!" Egan couldn't help complaining about the bumpy ride, and held on to his saddle horn for dear life. The road—which he couldn't see—might as well have been a hundred miles down, Egan imagined it so. He knew that if he fell, he would surely perish!

"Hush!" Sound traveled easily over the bogs. Billy was straining his ears to hear conversation or a sound of any kind from the travelers ahead, and he searched intently for the lights of their torches.

When he did see light on the road ahead, Billy reined in his ass—but too late, they were already at two torches stuck in the ground by the side of the road.

"Greetings, fellow travelers!" Sparano stepped out of the dark.

"Hello, sir," said a daunted Billy.

"What brings you out on a night like this?" Sparano was puzzled, he didn't expect to discover that it was two young men he had heard coming up behind.

Egan remembered that neither Sparano nor Campbell knew anything about St. Joseph's Monastery, and so he sidestepped the truth.

"We're on our way to St. Joseph's."

Sparano approached the lads for a better look. "I've been waiting here for someone," he lied, to justify his presence on the road. "What business would you have at the monastery?"

Egan thought quickly. "To give a message to someone, sir."

"And who might that be?"

Egan was hard pressed. "Brother . . . Fry. Brother William Fry."

"I don't remember any Brother William living at the monastery."

Egan relaxed a little. It was obvious Sparano was fishing, so Egan let his naturally active imagination run. "Oh, you know Brother William, sir. He's the little fellow with the big nose, kind of ugly?"

"He ain't so ugly," said Billy, regaining some of his lost composure.

"Where are you two gentlemen from?" asked Sparano.

"We work for Governor Gomez, sir, in the stables," Billy said, before Egan could again say something disparaging about Brother William.

"What kind of message would the governor trust two stable boys with?"

"Just that he wants to talk to Brother William," said Egan.

"About a matter of some urgency, I suspect," said Billy, "so we best be on our way now, sir, so we can do what we was told." Billy nodded his head in respect to Sparano while nudging his ass into motion.

"Good evening, sir," said Egan, following in Billy's wake.

The two lads left Sparano scratching his head, wondering what business the governor might have with Brother William. Could it have something to do with Lady Howard?

chapter 12

THE AMBUSH

Billy hurried his ass down the road a ways before pulling it to a stop.

"Get off your ass!" he yelled at Egan as he jumped off his.

They slapped the animals' haunches, sending them riderless to St. Joseph's. And then they hid in a tall patch of swamp grass growing beside the road, and waited.

Egan whispered, "What are we going to do when they get here?"

"We'll just have to take it as it comes," Billy whispered back.

"Best wait for the right time," Egan agreed. "We'll know it when it comes, so don't go rushing into anything."

"I'm not going to rush into anything!"

"You better not!" threatened Egan.

"Or what?"

"Or I'll excommunicate you, Brother William!"

Billy tore loose a fistful of grass and was about to toss it in Egan's face, when the muffled sound of ass hooves striking sand drifted up the road. The glow of the torches held by Sparano and Campbell, and then the ghostly silhouettes of the two men and Sarah on their mounts slowly emerged from the mist.

Sparano was in front. Campbell led Sarah's ass by a rope.

Billy and Egan fought the urge to spring out at Sarah's captors as they passed by. The two lads had to stay their ground because there was too much distance to cover for an ambush; they were lying flat on their bellies with only a small dagger apiece for weapons. Sparano and Campbell would see them coming for sure and have their sabers out and ready for the two to impale themselves upon.

So Billy and Egan let them pass.

But they started following closely behind, waiting for their chance.

For more than a mile, Billy and Egan followed on foot, with as much patience as they could muster.

Sparano finally stopped. They had come to the fork in the road that Foote had told Sparano about back at the stables. Here, only a short, steep embankment separated the road from the swamp.

"What's the problem, mate?" Campbell wanted to know why Sparano had dismounted.

"My muscles cry out for relief," Sparano said in his oily voice. "I'm sure the lady is feeling discomfort, too. Please help her down. I'll see what the signs say." Sparano carried his torch over to a signpost that had a sign pointing down each of the three intersecting directions: St. Pierre, St. Joseph, and Port of Spain. Holding high his torch, Sparano looked out across the swamp beyond the signpost.

Campbell helped Lady Howard, still bound and gagged, off her mount. Then he picked up the torch that he had stuck in the ground before . . .

"You grab the lady!" Billy yelled as he and Egan came running.

Billy crashed head-on into the chest of Jason Campbell, and they fell tumbling in a knot down the bank to the swamp.

"Come on!" Egan shouted, grabbing hold of Sarah.

At first Sarah felt only terror! Who was this new captor? But then she recognized the impetuous young man with his hand around her bound wrists. And back down the road they ran, as fast as Sarah could manage.

Sparano was startled by a flash of light. When Campbell and Billy fell into the swamp, Campbell's torch had flown from his hand and hit a pocket of methane gas bubbling up from below. A surging burst of flames roared across the swamp. For a moment, the swamp seemed to be illuminated by the rays of the sun. But it was soon night again, and darker than before—with the methane rapidly burning up and Campbell's torch sinking.

Now there was only Sparano's torch to see by.

The frightened asses were already in full gallop heading for St. Joseph's Monastery when Sparano took off running in the opposite direction after Egan and Sarah.

It was pitch black in the swamp as Billy tried to untangle himself from Jason Campbell. The water was waist deep where they wrestled. Billy reached for his dagger but found it had gotten lost in his fall into the swamp. He pushed Campbell away and scrambled for the road. Campbell made a grab in the dark for Billy's feet, found a foot, and started dragging the lad back into deeper water to drown him. Billy made a desperate jab at Campbell, swinging his fist in the dark at where he guessed the henchman's head to be, but he accidentally hit Campbell in the throat—smashing his windpipe!

Campbell let go of his hold and started thrashing about frantically like a fish in shallow water, struggling to breathe. Billy, aghast, slowly backed away, listening to the violently churning water gradually settle, as Jason Campbell expired.

When all was still, Billy clambered out of the swamp onto the road, and emptied his boots of water before running in the dark after the others.

Meanwhile, Egan pulled Sarah off the road.

"What's going on!" was the first thing Sarah said when

166

Egan removed her gag.

"Shhh! Stay low," Egan whispered. He untied Sarah's hands and wished there were more than swamp grass and a few scrawny trees and bushes to hide behind.

Soon the flare of Sparano's torch could be seen coming down the road. The henchman passed Sarah and Egan at a run, but shortly thereafter he came to a stop and started sweeping the road with his torch, back and forth.

"He's looking for our footprints," whispered Egan.

Sparano made his way back to where Egan and Sarah had left the road.

"We've got to get out of here," Egan whispered, and he and Sarah started backing up, deeper into what was fast turning into soggy marsh beneath their feet.

And then they heard Billy come sloshing down the road in his wet boots and clothes, and saw him stop when he came into view of Sparano.

"Whoa!" Billy yowled involuntarily, turning around.

Sparano unsheathed his saber and started after Billy.

"Come on," said Egan. He and Sarah returned to the road and ran for the safety of Port of Spain—still some three miles in the distance.

Sparano was a strong runner, in excellent health. But Billy had the vitality of youth on his side, and the adrenaline rush through his veins that fuels the hunted—be it human or squirrel—in the heat of a life-and-death chase.

Billy stumbled and almost fell into a dip in the road. Sparano gained on him, but not by much.

"Blast!" Sparano cursed as he came to a halt five minutes into the chase. He had expected to overrun the young man, kill him quickly, and then go back after the other two. But he had wasted too much time and energy—more than he should have allowed himself! He turned around and started again after the more important prey.

When Billy realized he was no longer being chased, he stopped and took off his boots. His boots had been filling with water dripping down from his wet clothes. The leather had become heavy, flaccid, and cumbersome. He carried his boots in his hands as he ran faster now, barefoot.

It didn't take him long to catch up with Sparano. The would-be assassin was scanning the road as he went, checking footprints, running slower than he had after Billy.

Sarah and Egan had been running without a stop, except for when they tripped and fell—something they both had done a couple of times since they started. "I can't go on!" gasped Sarah, falling to her knees, out of breath and about to faint.

"It can't be much farther, ma'am," Egan panted, also in need of a rest. He gave Sarah a moment to catch her breath before insisting they continue. Egan thought about hiding again, but he knew it would be only a matter of time before Sparano tracked them down. He hoped Billy had delayed Sparano long enough—tripped him up somehow.

Billy was thinking about attacking Sparano, but what good would that do? He was no match for Foote's henchman! Without even a dagger to fight with, Sparano would kill him easily and then be right after Egan and Sarah again! What could he do?

Billy, just behind Sparano, slowed down after seeing Sparano come to a sudden stop and cock his head as though he were listening to something. And then the henchman took off running at full speed.

Sparano must have heard Egan and Sarah! Billy ran as fast as he could after the villain—he had to stop him somehow!

"Hey, Sparano!" he called out, trying to get Sparano to chase him again. But Sparano continued running as if he didn't hear the challenge.

Billy's side began to ache as if it had been stabbed, but he kept on running as fast as he could in spite of the horrible cramp and with two lungs ready to burst. He threw one of his boots at Sparano, just missing his head. But Sparano ignored it! Billy threw the other boot and hit Sparano squarely in the back, but the bad man wouldn't even stagger.

Sparano! You son of a Carp! Billy tried to scream, but

his body was using all the air it could take in to breathe, there was none to spare for the luxury of words.

Billy was gaining on the henchman, steadily drawing near; but at the same time, his consciousness was deserting him, his awareness dimming, his vision fading. Billy made a desperate, collapsing dive in a final reach for Sparano. But he fell far, far short, into unconsciousness.

"Look!" said Egan, who had been pulling Sarah along to keep her going. "Light!"

The mist ahead was illuminated by the lights of Port of Spain.

"We're almost there!" he encouraged her, trying to inspire himself as well as Sarah. Egan had never been so exhausted. If it weren't for the sake of Her Ladyship, he would have given up the run long ago!

Sarah was numb; she had lost all sense of herself as she stumbled on. She was being propelled solely by the implacable will of Egan Shaw.

Egan could see the outlines of buildings now.

And then he and Her Ladyship were in an alley.

"We've made it," he said, "almost." He pulled on Sarah's limp arm. "Just a little farther."

And then behind them, rapidly approaching, Egan saw the glow of Sparano's torch.

"No!" Egan screamed. He got behind Sarah and gave her one last push toward the light, before passing out.

chapter 13

A PROMISE KEPT

Maxwell and his men headed for the governor's residence upon entering Port of Spain. Governor Manuel Gomez's home stood beside the ruins of a partially completed castle in the northeast of town. The governor was always glad to see Captain Maxwell.

Manuel Gomez was always glad to see anybody!

It had been more than five years since a Spanish ship had visited Port of Spain in any official capacity, and that was seven years after the one before that. The only contact Manuel had with the world outside Trinidad came by way of pirate ship, or the occasional merchant vessel that would drop a heavy anchor in Port of Spain's lonesome, fog-enveloped harbor.

"Capitan!" Manuel greeted Jacob Maxwell with open arms as the captain and his men were brought into the library by Manuel's slave and best friend, Samson.

The governor was standing before a long cherry-wood table, between two of a half-dozen tall rows of old and well-perused books.

Spread out on the table in a disheveled array were the yellowed, timeworn construction plans of a Spanish castle. Manuel had discovered his great-grandfather's plans as a child exploring the library. He would come here often to escape the often-dreary existence of Trinidad. The future governor spent many happy hours among the books, learning of distant lands, other times and possibilities.

"How is it coming along?" Maxwell asked, approaching the table.

"Maravilloso!" Manuel proudly proclaimed in his native tongue. He pointed at the drawing of what would one day be an antechamber of the castle. "Samson and I have been working here. We will soon have the walls, and then a section of roof—the first of the castillo!"

It was Manuel and Samson's custom to retire to the library after dinner and muse over the construction plans: discuss the work they were doing and argue about what should be done next.

In Manuel and Samson's many hours of spare time, they would labor at completing the castle, one stone at a time, using rocks that they blasted out of the abandoned quarry in the Northern Range. The governor once calculated that at the rate they were going, he and Samson would have the castle completed in the year 3026.

Manuel had other slaves who would help with the building of the castle, if asked—which he did once, but

Manuel could tell they weren't as enthusiastic about the project as he and Samson. He didn't want his slaves to become unhappy and run away, so he never asked them again. There wasn't a rush to finish the job anyhow—that wasn't the idea!

"You must come and see what we've done, tomorrow, when it is light." The only thing Manuel Gomez enjoyed more than building his castle was showing visitors what he and Samson had accomplished so far.

"I'm looking forward to it," said Maxwell, before changing the subject.

"Are there any ships in port, besides ours?"

"Si! Quite a few as a matter of fact." It was a rare occasion to have a ship anchored offshore, remarkable to have two. With the *Bernadette* there were now three ships in the Mouth of the Dragon. And two English vessels had come and gone in the past week.

Manuel was in much the same boat as Codfish Oglesby, the tavern owner in Nassau; the governor of Trinidad found it necessary to overlook most of what went on on his island or run the risk of being excluded from everything. At present, there was something big afoot in Port of Spain that no one had bothered to tell him about.

Maxwell told Manuel about Sarah Howard's abduction, and his desire to rescue her.

"Si, that explains much!" said Manuel, grateful for the

information. "Everyone is so . . . so to themselves—mucho misterioso!" He told Maxwell the names of the ships he knew were in port, and some of the men he had seen in town: the *Mary Ann* and the *Rhinehart*; captains Billy Beaumont, Gavette, and Delcarpio.

After a taste of the governor's finest sherry, some musings of Europe, and a toast to better weather, Maxwell and his men continued on their quest for the Lady Howard.

They had just come out of a tavern and were heading for another when they happened upon Russell Gavette and a band of his men—accompanied by Armand Delcarpio—coming down the street opposite them.

The buccaneers fell back a step behind their respective leaders, letting Maxwell and Gavette be the first to meet, knowing that it was up to the two captains to decide the matters needing to be discussed, aware that the fates of everyone concerned were bound up with this confrontation.

And so the time had finally come, the one facing the other, man to man, Maxwell and Gavette!

"I see you've sunk to stealing favors and petticoats, Captain Gavette," Jacob accused his former best friend.

"No, you speak of yourself, Captain Maxwell," answered Russell.

"No, I was speaking of deceit, of a lack of honor, and of

low-handed treachery."

"And again you describe your own character with such remarkable accuracy, leaving out only the perception of a mole, the courage of a fowl, and the deductive reasoning of a noseless gutter rat!"

Maxwell drew his sword. "And now I believe it is your misfortune that I prove you to be the loathsome, lying villain that you are!"

As young men, Jacob and Russell practiced the art of sword fighting by fencing each other. Over time, they had created a routine: a succession of well-calculated and perfectly-timed steps, sidesteps, stabs and counterblows, thrusts and parries. Techniques were added, withdrawn, and improved upon; so when the time came that they had to use their skills in a real life situation, they were well prepared and victorious. Their reputations spread fast and far, and not only for their outstanding abilities with a sword, but also for their keen minds, and for their leadership.

Now, thousands of miles from where Jacob and Russell had first tested each other's steel, in a foggy night on a street of dirty sand, the two went through their drill one last time, not missing a step, although it had been years since they had executed the mock duel.

The other men stood back and looked on with admiration at a marvelous performance that culminated with

crossed swords at close range—with the duelists standing nose to nose, chest to chest.

"And now for the real thing!" hissed Maxwell into the
face of Gavette.

They pushed each other off, and were about to go at
each other in earnest, when they were interrupted by a
shout from the alley in front of which they were dueling;
they looked to see Egan Shaw give Lady Howard a shove
out of the mist; she stumbled and fell to the ground at
their feet.

And after the lady, also from nowhere, Frederick Sparano came running. Foote's henchman tossed his torch
aside and drew his saber.

Realizing all was lost when he saw the two captains
and their men, Sparano elected to die in battle rather than
rot away in a cage or swing at the end of some ignoble
rope.

"He is mine!" shouted Maxwell, claiming the honor.

Sparano would have been a better match for Maxwell
if he hadn't been so exhausted from his run. Sweating
profusely, gasping for breath, and staggering on legs of
lead, he made a reckless swipe of his sword at the captain
of the *Bernadette*.

Maxwell was reluctant to take advantage of the handi-
capped warrior, thinking it would be more honorable to
let Sparano rest up a bit—give him a fair chance. But

then again, this brute was about to do harm to—if not kill—young Egan Shaw! And what about Her Ladyship?

The captain resolved to do Foote's henchman in. He forced the exhausted Sparano backward with a series of powerful strokes. Sparano stumbled and fell, and Maxwell was about to end the short battle . . .

"Stop, Captain!" yelled Egan, pulling himself up off of the ground, regaining his senses. "Don't kill him! We need what he knows!"

"Very well." Maxwell knocked Sparano's sword from him with the last of a flurry of slashes. The defeated villain was then surrounded by Maxwell's crew.

"Tell us what you know," Maxwell demanded of his prisoner, placing his blade under the henchman's chin, lifting the jaded, listless face.

Sparano managed a subdued but sincere growl, expressing a willingness to die rather than betray a confidentiality.

Maxwell turned and addressed Egan, who was now at Sarah's side, helping her up, "*You* tell us what *you* know!"

Maxwell and his men and Sarah moved from the street to the nearest tavern.

Gavette and his men withdrew. The score between the captains of the *Bernadette* and the *Rhinehart* would have to be settled another time, this opportunity had come undone.

Egan downed most of his first pint of ale in one breath before beginning his story. Halfway into the telling, Billy Fry arrived, barefoot, and helped Egan finish the tale.

"Are you sure Foote said Dudley? Albert Dudley?" Sarah couldn't believe it when Egan related the conversation he and Billy had overheard between Razmus Foote and Frederick Sparano in the livery stable.

"He just said Dudley, ma'am," said Egan. "There wasn't no Albert."

Billy confirmed this.

Sarah shook her head. "But why would Albert Dudley want to kill me? We were to be married!"

"Maybe Foote was referrin' to Lord Robert Dudley, his uncle," offered Toby Gant.

"Or maybe it was another Dudley altogether," speculated Moon.

"I'd have to think it was the uncle or the nephew, or both," said Maxwell. "To be certain we'll have to find Razmus Foote."

Maxwell left Sparano and Sarah in the care of Governor Gomez, and then he and his men made a thorough search of Port of Spain. But they found not a trace of Foote, anywhere.

"He probably disappeared into the swamp," said Spike.

"Most likely the devil's home," agreed the captain.

chapter 14

TYBURN FAIR

Certain that Razmus Foote was nowhere to be found, Maxwell ordered everybody back to the ship; he wanted to sail before anything else went wrong. In the short time before dawn, until the galleon was truly under way, the anxious captain paced back and forth between the rails of the *Bernadette*, prepared to receive unwanted visitors with the sharp end of his sword.

It was a forty-day sail to England on the Gulf Stream, giving Sarah and Rebecca plenty of time to get to know the crew of the *Bernadette*. Sarah became especially fond of Egan and Billy, and the two lads did little to dissuade Her Ladyship's kind regards.

Rebecca did her best to convince Jacob Maxwell that not all people born of privilege were necessarily predisposed to doing evil.

The captain, however, found Rebecca considerably

more attractive now that she was no longer breathing royal air.

Queen Elizabeth was shocked to hear that someone named Dudley might be involved with the kidnapping of her cousin, and she kept her distance from Robert until the matter could be resolved.

Robert's nephew, Albert, was taken in chains to the royal dungeon for questioning. He was led down a long, dark and dreary passage of stone steps and rock walls, passing row after row of dingy cells and wretched creatures— some hardly recognizable as human. At the bottom of the underground prison lay a torture chamber. Albert was strapped to the rack next to Frederick Sparano, who had already been stretching there awhile.

A large and black-hooded fellow gave a tug on the crank at Sparano's feet in honor of Albert's arrival. Sparano's agonizing scream clawed at the walls of the torture chamber.

Finding the fate of being slowly pulled apart much too undignified a way to die, Lord Dudley's nephew promised to confess to the kidnapping of Lady Howard just as soon as someone could guarantee him a fast and merciful exit from the world.

Albert, it seems, had used his position as Robert Dudley's nephew to extort large sums of money and invest it in businesses considered unsavory by the queen.

He owned a couple of profitable but illegal gambling establishments; this required someone enjoying the blessing of the royal court, and Albert had convinced whoever needed to know that this was indeed his prerogative.

When his meddling uncle and Queen Elizabeth ordered him to get married, Albert panicked. The wonderful life he was living, the life he had worked so hard to create for himself, could not go on under the noses of the Howards. So he arranged for the kidnapping and removal of Lady Howard to Trinidad until he could decide what to do with her. His first thought was to ransom Sarah to compensate for everything he was going to have to give up; but soon after the news of the kidnapping reached him, Albert changed his mind. He decided that the best solution to his problem would be to remove Sarah altogether. He sent a message to his man in the islands, Razmus Foote, on the next ship sailing for the Caribbean: Her Ladyship was to be discreetly done away with.

Albert Dudley and Frederick Sparano were to be hanged the day after Albert confessed. Albert's confession was made on a Monday, and Tuesday was hanging day.

A large crowd turned out at Tyburn Fair to witness the execution. The Tuesday hangings were always a popular event, but with Lord Dudley's nephew being put to the rope, there was a good chance folks might be able to see the Virgin Queen herself come to watch.

Jacob Maxwell took Rebecca Webb to Tyburn Fair for the hanging, and showed her the best place to view the spectacle, on a rooftop near the gallows and above the crowd, where Jacob and Russell had often come as boys with their gang.

"We'll have a good look at the crowd as well as the criminals being hanged," explained Jacob. "The crowd is more fun to watch than those at the ends of their ropes; when you have someone famous up there dangling, the crowd goes crazy. They start pushin' and shovin' and yellin' to get a better look. We used to wager on how many people would be crushed to death come the end of the day."

"That's disgusting!" objected Rebecca.

"Well, yes and no," Jacob defended himself. "It would depend on who was being done away with, now wouldn't it? You take some good-for-nothing that did you or your kind harm: you're happy to see 'em swing. Now, if it's a mate of yours that's been framed or wrongfully judged, then you hope he takes a few vultures along with him when he goes."

"Vultures?"

"Those." Jacob pointed a finger at the front of the crowd, at the people nearest the gallows.

The first five to be hanged this Tuesday were led onto the platform and fitted with nooses. The crowd began to jabber, the loudest being the vultures in front. Rebecca watched them taunt the condemned, yell at one another, and exchange money.

"Why are they passing around money?" asked Rebecca.

"They're making their wagers."

"What could they possibly be betting on?"

"All sorts of things. You have the first one and the last one to stop twitching—that's the popular bet. Then you have the man who faints before the trap is sprung, those who shed tears and claim everybody is making a big mistake, and those who see the wickedness of their ways at last and start begging for forgiveness. You name a situation and there's somebody down there betting on it every which way."

The condemned were allowed a few last words to explain themselves, during which time it was hard to hear what they were saying above the fluttering vultures. But when the traps were sprung and the five fell to their deaths, a hush came over Tyburn Fair, and it remained quiet until a doctor pronounced the five departed. Then, from the crowd, there arose a blend of righteous clapping and timely remarks.

"Well, look here!" exclaimed Jacob, when the next group was being ushered onto the platform. "If it ain't Ansel Potts! Ansel was in our gang, way back when. He used to sit up here where we are now."

Ansel Potts noticed Jacob and smiled sheepishly. They were too far apart to hear each other over the murmuring crowd, but Maxwell shrugged his shoulders and called out to him.

"What happened?"

Ansel shook his head and mouthed his words: Bad luck!

Ansel gave Jacob a wink when it was his turn to speak his last. He cursed England and all her subjects. Ansel poured it on particularly thick concerning the vultures in the front rows, calling them what they were: the devil's own and worse. The vultures shouted back names at him in retaliation, and threw wads of paper, sticks, pebbles, apple cores, and tomatoes. By the time the traps were sprung and the convicts fell, the crowd was in a real tizzy. There wasn't a moment of silence this time to acknowledge the passing of the condemned. The crowd was bustling—pushing and shoving in all directions. When soldiers finally calmed everybody down, many folks remained where they lay, trampled.

"Looks like old Ansel came out ahead in the end, now doesn't it!" Jacob laughed. "That's a few less vultures to bother with from now on."

Rebecca was appalled. "He did that intentionally! Riling the crowd!"

"That he did! And a right smart job of it!"

The injured, dying and dead were dragged from the

fair as the next lot were fitted with ropes; counted among these were Albert Dudley and Frederick Sparano. Sparano had to be helped to his hanging by a couple of guards; his legs had been too badly damaged on the rack for him to walk unaided.

"Does this happen often?" asked Rebecca.

"What's that?"

"The crowd getting out of control."

"Often enough, I suppose."

"But why bother if you know you're going to be hurt?"

"I doubt that they do know—too caught up in the sport of it, most likely."

Albert Dudley broke down sobbing when it was his time to speak. Several women in the audience wept along with him, and they yelled at the horrible sheriff to let the obviously innocent man go, even though a good many of them had no idea which Dudley he was, and they would be forgetting all about him three hours hence.

When it was his time to speak, Sparano only spat.

* * *

When Jacob Maxwell was given a queen's commission, it wasn't the gala the captain had expected and halfheartedly desired. Instead of a mighty fanfare in a great hall, there were but a few members of court in the queen's chancellor's office. But the Virgin Queen did attend, and she spoke to Jacob, who found himself bowing with sincerity for the first time in his life.

"We are most pleased to make your acquaintance," said Queen Elizabeth. She ceremoniously impressed the document with hot wax and then elegantly handed it to the proud captain. "May you continue to serve your country in the noble spirit you have displayed in the rescue of my dear cousin. Godspeed to you and your ship."

The queen's dear cousin, Sarah, made Egan and Billy's visit to England one to remember. She invited them to Howard House, the family's country estate outside London, where the two lads stayed in luxury. Sarah and Billy tried to teach Egan to ride a horse, but Egan found an English saddle even more difficult to stay in than the one on the back of the hard-trotting ass in Trinidad. And then there were the feasts of tiny birds in sweet gravies. And the trips to the theater and the opera.

Billy and Egan appreciated Sarah's generosity. They found much of her world intriguing if not magical at times. But, alas, it wasn't their world in the end, and they were not altogether sorry to get word one afternoon that the *Bernadette* would be sailing in the morning.

Sarah and Rebecca waved farewell from shore as the *Bernadette*, proudly flying the Union Jack, eased out of the harbor.

It was a new beginning for the *Bernadette*. The British Navy was now an ally, although it was going to be difficult for most English naval officers to accept the friendly status of Maxwell and his horde, and many were going to do their best to find an excuse to break the trust.

The waters of Europe and the Mediterranean were now more accessible to the *Bernadette*, as well as the coasts of Africa and Asia. Maxwell felt the whole world was now within his reach, and he was eager to test his good fortune. Perhaps he would sail to Madagascar and visit his old mentor, Captain Thatch Fitz-Henry. Or lay siege to a Peruvian port city on the west coast of South America—something Maxwell had always wanted to try. And now he could! And would!

But first he had to make a quick strike to replenish the *Bernadette*'s dwindling swag; the men were out of funds after their long stay in England.

Maxwell was hoping the first ship they encountered on the Atlantic crossing would be a nice, fat, treasure-laden Spanish galleon, traveling alone. But this was unlikely: Spanish treasure ships sailed in armadas, escorted by warships. The only time a treasure galleon was found by herself was when she was on her way to or from an armada, or when she became separated from her sister ships in a gale.

It was a brig, a two-masted Dutch merchantman, that

the *Bernadette* first came across, its hold most likely full of North American animal hides.

The *Bernadette* came abreast the smaller vessel and demanded she submit by firing the obligatory cannon ball across her bow.

To Maxwell's surprise, the little ship refused to yield. Perhaps this Dutch vessel was returning from the Dutch East Indies with a fortune in spice in her hold! Some spices were worth more than their weight in gold. But it was usually the larger three-masted galleons that carried spice, and they sailed in armadas.

Had this brig gotten lost?

"She must be carrying a fine prize, lads!" shouted Maxwell, "Why else fight a battle she knows she must lose?"

It was a good fight. The crew of the Dutch brig were well disciplined, and determined. Maxwell complimented the ship's captain for running a fine, tight ship when the Dutchman finally surrendered.

"Attention, lads!" Maxwell yelled from the deck of the conquered vessel so all could hear. "Any Englishmen aboard this brig, willing to join the *Bernadette*? We'll be needing a few new mates."

"It looks like four new mates, Cap'n," said Quartermaster Fenton. "Remember, we lost Dugan and Harper at Port Royal."

Maxwell walked over to where one of his men, now

dead, was being tossed over the side.

"Who bested this man? There goes a fine mate!" announced the captain as the lifeless body hit the water with a splash. "A swashbucklin' picaroon if ever there was!"

"That's your man, Cap'n," Ivy Sabin shouted from his perch atop the *Bernadette*. Ivy was pointing at a buccaneer not far from where Maxwell was standing: a tall, lanky, and red-bearded fellow with his hand raised.

"You're an Englishman? Loyal to the queen?"

"Aye, sir!"

"How would you like to sail with the *Bernadette*, the finest ship to ever sail the seven seas!"

"I would like that, Cap'n. Be much obliged!"

"What's your name, then?"

"Winston Smith of Wales, sir," said the man.

"No! No!" exclaimed Maxwell. "That'll never do!" The captain turned and stepped to the rail of the Dutch merchantman, and looked out over the sea. The dead from both ships were slowly floating away, dispersing out into the great immensity of the Atlantic Ocean.

"That name will never do aboard the *Bernadette*! I'm giving you the name of the man you dispatched. A fine mate! An honor to have at your side in any battle!"

Maxwell turned back to the new recruit and faced him squarely.

"Welcome aboard, Toby Gant!"